The Blessing of Pequea Sam

J. B. FISHER

WESTBOW
PRESS®
A DIVISION OF THOMAS NELSON
& ZONDERVAN

WestBow Press books may be ordered through booksellers or by contacting:

WestBow Press
A Division of Thomas Nelson & Zondervan
1663 Liberty Drive
Bloomington, IN 47403
www.westbowpress.com
1 (866) 928-1240

ISBN: 978-1-5127-5960-0 (sc)
ISBN: 978-1-5127-5961-7 (hc)
ISBN: 978-1-5127-5959-4 (e)

Library of Congress Control Number: 2016916713

Print information available on the last page.

WestBow Press rev. date: 3/8/2017

Contents

Dedication

To Amy Fisher Mathison, beloved daughter and friend, who is named after Amos Henry Fisher, descendant of Pequea Sam, the hero of this story. I dedicate this book to you and yours: Gregory, Olivia, Ashlyn and Broderick.

Acknowledgements

I gratefully acknowledge the following:

My Kamehameha School writing students who
taught me more than I ever taught them;

The nurses and therapists at Hale Ho'ola
Hamakua, Rehab Hospital, who taught me to
laugh rather than to feel sorry for myself;

Lydia Blank, my faithful and caring sister, who encouraged me
to continue writing despite grappling with a major disability;

Mark Conrad, Lynn Williams, Ab Hershberger, and
Ken Hoober, loyal college classmates, who stood
by me and urged me to "get the job done."

Duane Uyetake and his maintenance crew who pampered me and
helped me to work through many difficulties and technicalities;

Levi Fisher, "cousin Terry", for looking into archives in
the Lancaster County Courthouse and diverse libraries so
that I was able to stick to the truth whenever possible;

Don Yoder, University of Pennsylvania Professor,
for writing such an "akamai" *Introduction;*

All the help from the friends at the Life Care Center of Hilo,
especially Rachel Goldberg, who was my virtual "brains"

And for all the loyal folks at WestBow Press.

Foreword

On writing: Conjuring words out of my head and turning them into black marks on paper is somehow very exciting to me and is a great privilege for which I am truly grateful.

Writing a book is an adventure. At first it becomes like a mistress, then a master and finally a monster. For this last phase, you kill the monster and fling it to the public. *(Sir Winston Churchhill)*

I agree with Mark Twain who said that truth is stranger than fiction, that fiction is obliged to possibilies where truth isn't. As to *this writng* I present it as part fiction and part truth. Some parts rely upon the writer's conjecture because their contents are "hidden from record."

Introduction

By Dr. Don Yoder, Professor Emeritus of Folklife Studies and Religious Studies at the University of Pennsylvania.

This is the story of two brothers, twin-born in the Old Country, the elder of whom through trickery, abetted by his stepmother, receives from his dying father the Blessing of the Forefathers, intended, by long tradition, for the younger son. The strong Biblical underlay points to the Old Testament story of the Patriarch Jacob receiving, also through trickery, the parental blessing intended for his older brother Esau *(Genesis chapter 27)*. So the book becomes a sermon on forgiveness, played out in the lives of two very human Amish brothers, who wrestle with their guilt in the Old Country, where the tainted blessing took place, and in the New World, where each brother faces his own destiny.

The book is indeed a gripping recital of how festering hatred can destroy a family. Far from idealizing the Amish, as most works geared to the current tourist trade do, it gives a frank portrayal of the common and widespread faults of the Amish people, whose religion based in its <u>Ordnung</u> of rigid and iron-clad do's and dont's, is legalistic, judgmental, and often self-righteous. Pinpointed as a common trouble-maker in the community is gossip, an especial gift of Amish women.

To this serious and well-portrayed moralism, comic relief is provided by several obvious anachronisms introduced (I believe intentionally) by the author. One is the 20th century trolley line that takes the protagonists into town (Lancaster) on various missions. Another is the promotion of Lancaster town to city status, which it did not reach until later, after first graduating into borough status in 1742. At any rate, these anachrorisms are amusing, and in a sense turn the book into very readable fantasy fiction. But the serious core of the book is the wrestling with guilt over the misappropriated blessing by both the brothers, in Europe and the New World. One of them (the charismatic Pequea Sam) appears to have reached full forgiveness, while his self-righteous brother (Preacher Jacob) festers his life away, forgiving his brother outwardly – with his lips, but not in his heart.

The book is readable throughout - the author knows how to tell a good story - and will make a useful addition to the growing corpus of Amish literature. This is especially the case since the theme of forgiveness has surfaced in books, as a result of the unfortunate terrorist attack on a Lancaster County Amish school several years ago. Forgiveness is always there in the Amish world as an ideal, but its treatment in this book shows how difficult it is to achieve, especially in a divided family.

In Pennsylvania Dutch culture, when a farmer father comes to the decisive point of "retirement," it was customary for him to give the farm to his youngest son, having provided for older sons earlier in his career. This was a custom brought across the Atlantic by our Swiss ancestors, who in practicing it were following the laws of their ancestral Canton of Bern, which favored the youngest son. This is the opposite practice to primogeniture, which in some European areas favored the first-born or eldest son. In Pennsylvania, when the farm was transferred, the son got the farmhouse and was obligated to build a Grossdaddihaus for the parents, where they could live separately and work at their own pace. They never really retired completely! One of their self-designated tasks was to supervise their grandchildren, and pass on to them the traditions of the family and community. Most of the Pennsylvania Dutch people followed this custom in Pennsylvania – although today the Amish are among the last full practitioners in carrying it out – complete to the Grossdaddihaus that we see on most Amish farms. The custom also had the practical benefit of separating the two families, and avoiding mother-in-law and daughter-in-law conflicts. In witness whereof, let me quote a time-honored Pennsylvania proverb: "No house is big enough for two families."

In its presentation of Amish life and culture to the reader, the book mercifully spares us from such tourist-literature claims like the one attributing the invention of the "whoopee-pie" to the Amish. Actually, while it has been adopted by the Amish, it can today be considered Amish, it is a Yankee invention from Massachusetts, that made its way into the Amish world, first in the Midwest, and then in Pennsylvania. Its fatuous, flippant name decidedly conflicts with the Amish emphasis on self-control, diligently avoiding the making of "whoopee" in any actions of one's life.

But this excursus enables me to point out that the same adoptive process is actually true of most of the Amish culture as we have it today. Most of its elements were absorbed from the majority culture of the so-called Kirchenleute or "church people" – i.e., the Lutherans and Reformed, the two major religious traditions of the Protestant Reformation, whose settlements bordered or surrounded the Amish everywhere. In Pennsylvania the "church people" formed at least 80% of the Pennsylvania Dutch population, while the Sektenleute or "plain people" (Mennonites, Brethren, Amish, and others) represented only 20% of the whole. And where today the Amish stand out in many ways as "different" from the majority Dutch, in 1900, before the automobile took over, the look and culture of the two groups were just not that different. Most Pennsylvania Dutchmen then, Amish or not, wore beards – in the late 19th and early 20th centuries - in part a result of the cultural upheavals of the Civil War, which had a long-lasting effect in changing Dutch customs and attitudes.

The many nice notes in the book include the portrayal of the neighoring Pequea and Susquehannock Indians - in the period of the Amish settlement - as human beings. The portrayal of Amish childhood, in the example of Pequea Sam's "heel-trotter" nephew, Sammy II, is also refreshing and pleasant, with some of the book's action viewed through Sammy II's growing perception of life. All this points up the importance of role models within the family, and lifelong loyalty of family members to each other – not always the case but when it happens, it is always memorable. And best of all as a character sketch of a non-Amish person is the author's winsome portrayal of the ex-Quaker proprietress ("madam") of Lancaster's only colonial brothel, where one of the brothers (Pequea Sam) receives periodic mentoring with practical advice and creature comforts.

In the book, young Pequea Sam is described as having a red beard, an interesting physical characteristic that deserves explanation. I remember first seeing red-bearded Amishmen in the 1920s, on a trip with my father through Central Pennsylvania, when I was about five. In the Big Valley or Kishacoquillas Valley in Mifflin County, a major Amish settlement, we stopped to visit an Amish friend of his. Yes, he had a red beard, and the two friends talked Dutch – which at the time I could not understand, although I do today, and speak it with pleasure (<u>schwetz</u> <u>es mit</u> <u>Blessier</u>). The little boy evidently got restless, and the farmer's wife brought him, fresh from the oven, a half-moon pie, a Big Valley specialty.

Those Big Valley red beards were explained to me much later, when on an ethnographic visit to the area with John Hostetler, a Big Valley native, whose book, <u>Amish Society</u> (Johns Hopkins Press, 1952), is in my opinion still the best introduction to Amish life and culture. John told me that the red beards among the Amish there can be attributed to intermarriage with the Scotch-Irish, who were the original settlers of the valley, before the Amish (including families of Amish Yoders!) arrived in the 1790s. Of course Pequea Sam brought his red beard from the Old Country, so there must have been additional sources.

To elaborate, Yoder is an extremely widespread Amish surname, and while I have no Amish background at all in my family, I am happy to claim cousinship with the thousands of Old Order Amish who are Yoder descendants. John Hostetler himself told me that he had five Yoder lines in his family tree!

My Yoders were always <u>Kirchenleute</u>, Reformed Church adherents in Switzerland, the Palatinate, and Colonial Pennsylvania. The Amish Yoders split off in the 1690s from the main Reformed trunk of the family in Canton Bern, Switzerland, Alsace, and the Palatinate, and have been separate ever since. But as the Dutch put it, we are all in the same <u>Freindschaft</u> or extended family. And after this ramble into geneology, I must also report that I have never forgotten that welcome gift of the half-moon pie.

One final comment: the author has, alas, not enlightened his readers on how much of his story is based on truth, through family tradition, and how much is fiction. The Amish are a remembering people. They have long memories, and some families have recorded aspects of their earlier history in Europe, particularly scenes from those difficult days when they were persecuted in Switzerland and exiled to the "Lowlands" (Alsace, the Palatinate, and elsewhere in the Central Rhoneland). There, however, they ranked as second-class citizens, not always able to own their own land, but were lessees, with sometimes the hereditary right to pass the lease on to their children. The general term for such lease-holders is *Erbbestaender,* based on the legal term for the lease – *Erbbestandsbrief.*

In conclusion, let me make the statement, that the Amish, with all their virtues, yes, and all their faults as a people apart, with their Biblical reverence for the land and their Old Country - honed farming techniques, have been a major factor in making Lancaster County, Pennsylvania, what it has frequently been called in the 20th Century – the "Garden Spot of America."

Thank you, John Fisher, for your even-handed approach to the legacy of your own people, the Old Order Amish.

Dr. Don Yoder
August 7, 2015

Dr. Don Yoder, a University of Chicago Ph.D., is Professor Emeritus of Folklife Studies and Religious Studies at the University of Pennsylvania, where he taught for forty years (1956 – 1996). While there, he founded the graduate folklife studies program, the first in the nation, and directed fifty-three doctoral dissertations. Widely published, his books include, *Songs along the Mahantongo* (1951, 2nd ed. 1964), *Pennsylvania Spirituals (1961), American Folklife (1976), Pennsylvania German Immigrants (1980), Rhineland Immigrants (1982), Hex Signs 1989, 2nd ed. 2000), The Picture Bible of Ludwig Denig: A Pennsylvania German Emblem Book (2 vols., 1989), Discovering American Folklife (1990, 2nd ed. 2001), Amish Folk Medicine (1999), Ground Hog Day (2003)* and, *The Pennsulvania German Broadside(2005).* Forthcoming are *Introduction to the Amish,* and the conference volume *Ephemera Across the Atlantic: Popular Print Culture from Two Worlds,* the papers of the international conference he organized in 2005 for the Library Company of Philadelphia and Winterthur Museum.

Dr. Yoder's teaching and research specialties include American folklife, religion in America, sectarian culture, religious folksong, folk art and architecture, Quaker ethnography, and Pennsylvania Dutch studies. He was a founding trrustee of the American Folklife Center at the Library of Congress, and has served as President of the American Folklife Society. He has participated at international conferences in Sweden, Germany, Switzerland, italy, the Czech Republic, France, Romania, England, Wales, Ireland, the United States, and Canada. He was co-founder and editor of the journals *The Pennsylvania Dutchman (1949-1958)* and *Pennsylvania Folklife (1958-1978),* as well as editor of the Pennsylvania German Society's journal *Der Reggeboge / The Rainbow (1992-1996).* Finally, with two professors from Franklin and Marshall College, he was co-founder (in 1950) and co-director of the Pennsylvania Dutch Folk Festival at Kutztown, Pennsylvania, America's first folklife festival, still going strong after sixty years.

Prologue

$\mathfrak{I}$n the Old Country (*Das Alte Landt*), certain Jewish fathers observed *The Blessing of the Forefathers*—a generational rite of passage, in which a legacy was passed down by solemn bequest through a father to his youngest son. *"Because God loved you and kept the oath He swore to you as the meek to inherit the land. (Deuteronomy 7:6-9)*

Certain Old Order Amish fathers, with whom they held things in common with Jewish fathers in *Das Alte Landt*, observed the *Blessing* as well. In passing down the *Blessing*, the Old Order Amish father preserved the wisdom and lineage of his forefathers to an entitling son of his immediate generation. Those who observed the ritual believed it would survive for time immemorial.

"We do not own our land, we borrow it from our children," goes the Old Order Amish proverb. Thereupon, at his age of accountability, the son of entitlement was called upon to inherit the land, to care for it on behalf of his forefathers, then pass the land to the next generation through his own "entitling son."

The bestowing father placed an awesome responsibility down upon his son. For the entitling son to *pass up* the *Blessing* would be unpardonable; for him to *squander* the *Blessing* would be an abomination; but for him to *violate* the *Blessing* would bring on a spiritual banishment worse than death.

Part One
Das Alte Lande

Chapter 1

Genesis

The labor-weary farmer bent over the chipped agate basin of cistern water and lye soap. "Vell, vas is das?"the tired father asked Mary, the *maud*, splashing water over the back of his neck and into his long beard in one seeming motion.

"It's twins," the maid answered somewhat matter-of-factly, glancing up from her station at the cookstove.

A slab of lye soap slid heavily across the wooden kitchen floor. *"Zwei? Zwei!"*

"Two boys. The doctor said it was a *'pretty rough go'* for Mattie. She gave it all she could."

⊶⊷

Christian Fisher, a hard working Amish father, had hurried to the village to summon the doctor about his wife Mattie's agonizing birthing pains. Sensing the emergency, the good doctor pushed aside his plate of half-eaten supper, hitched up his own horse to his own surrey, and followed the expectant father back to his farm. The doctor hurried into the house to see what was up with Mattie, while Christian stayed in the barn to milk his cows and complete the evening barn chores.

In *Das Alte Landt* the Amish performed their work without the benefit of anything modern or "convenient." The peasant farmers lived simply, and they labored hard, singing of God and family. The families harvested their wheat by hand, and ground the kernels into a coarse flour to make their own bread. They milked their cows by hand, churned their own butter, and processed their own cheese.

The peasant people possessed a power born of persecution, like natural-born survivors. They were rugged individualists. Those in the outside seldom messed with them, and they kept to themselves.

⋄⊶≡◉ ◎≡⊷⋄

Samuel was born first. Like his father, he was large and swarthy, a difficult birth for such a woman. Jacob, slight and fair-haired like his mother, had grabbed onto his older brother's heel.

From the beginning, the mother remembered the agony the large and swarthy Samuel had brought her and resented him at her breast. She favored the slight and fair-haired Jacob. Already the infant Samuel would feel the sting of rejection.

Later on, after the frail and small-boned mother had not recovered from birthing her twin sons, Samuel felt the sting of rejection all over again.

⋄⊶≡◉ ◎≡⊷⋄

Mary, the *live-in maud,* took on the responsibity of raising the toddlers where the deceased mother had left off. Like their mother Mattie, Mary cherished the quiet, second-born Jacob and preferred him over Samuel the first-born. From the beginning, Jacob spent his days in the kitchen with the maud and naturally became house-bound.

Mary did not like having the rambunctious Samuel under foot. Every day she shooed him out of the house, where he walked behind the heels of his father, and that became a man of the field.

⋄⊶≡◉ ◎≡⊷⋄

The boys were eight when their father married for the second time. An assertive and controlling stepmother entered the picture. Family loyalties changed abruptly. The new mother favored the swarthy and rambunctious Samuel over the younger Jacob, because the older Samuel reminded her of her new husband. With the shifting of the stepmother's parental loyalties, life for everyone seemed to change rather suddenly and dramatically.

⁘⁘⁘

The day came when Christian Fisher was confined to his bed. He lay weak with a chill that struck his very heart. While he lay weak and ill, Samuel, the apple of the father's eye, never left by his ailing father's bedside.

On a particularly down day, Christian believed his spirit was about to leave him. He called his new wife to his bedside. "Listen carefully to my words, and obey my instruction. The day is coming for me to hand down the *blessing of my fathers.* By tradition, my youngest son, Jacob, will carry the wisdom and lineage of my fathers down to his generation."

"Bring the boy to me. Have him cross his arms and lay him upon my breast. I must pass the *Blessing* to him so that I can take my rest."

It was believed that the son of entitlement would walk the path of his forefathers. Samuel listened with great fear to the instruction which his ailing father gave to the stepmother. Bright beyond his age, the lad understood the tradition well enough to comprehend what was about to happen. Soon it would be his father's last day and he would face rejection once again.

The ailing father took pride in the family's tradition. He took great comfort in knowing that Jacob would become wise in walking the path of his forefathers. According to Genesis 25:23,

"The one shall be stronger than the other, and the elder shall serve the younger." Thereupon *Jacob*, mild man of the house, would inherit his father's kingdom, and *Samuel,* swarthy man of the field, would become his servant. Samuel, however, believed that since he was his father's favorite son, *he* would be the better suited to inherit the father's kingdom. Alas, the *blessing of the forefathers* would pass to his younger brother. Young Samuel felt the pain of rejection as never before. The pain of jealousy overcame his sensitive young spirit.

⬥⭢ ⭠⬥

The doting stepmother, however, perceived Samuel's pain and took the matter into her own hands. At her encouragement young Samuel crept into his father's bedroom. He crossed his arms upon his father's breast and stole Jacob's blessing for *himself.*

"My son, by my death, I hand my blessing down to you. From the depth of my soul I bless you, my youngest son, as you receive the blessing of my fathers. Receive the blessing well. You shall become wise by walking the path so long walked by your forefathers before you. In turn you will hand the blessing to your own youngest son, in like manner as I have this day handed it to you."

Thus was the *Blessing* of Christian Fisher's generation pronounced upon Samuel, and not upon the younger Jacob as the sacred tradition would have it; and thus was the *Blessing* tainted by a stepmother's deception, visiting a curse upon the Christian G. Fisher family through the third and fourth generation!

"You have blessed me above all others," Samuel whispered to his ailing father. *"I will at all times live worthy of your blessing."*

"But Samuel! But how can this be?" The father sat up, looked around, then fell back onto his bed, distraught that he had not been able to follow his father's tradition.

"It was I who placed Samuel upon your breast," lied the stepmother, protecting the son she favored.

"You? You have just brought a curse upon my generation!" the stricken husband wailed. "There can be no way for mortal man to set right the wrong you have committed! You have confounded my generation and sent me to an early grave!"

The ailing man despised his wife and turned against her. In like manner the stepmother turned against Samuel, who now would have to spend the rest of his life trying to prove himself worthy of the blessing which he had received by his stepmother's deceit. At the same time Jacob, the innocent one, had to bear the torment of his family's curse.

⊶⊜ ⊜⊷

Jacob wished for all the world to forgive his brother for stealing the blessing from him. However, after he realized that was no way to come against the family's curse, he knew that forgiveness would not come easily. The curse which had confounded his generation also demonized the brothers, who were destined to live like a family accursed.

The one most affected by the deceit was Christian Fisher himself. For the ailing husband and father, the die was cast, the hammer down. Despair settled over everything. The once-proud man gave up on everything that mattered, after he realized he had not upheld the sacred tradition around the *blessing of the forefathers*.

Christian Fisher, high-strung and fiercely self-righteous, had set his sons up to fail. The brothers appeared caught up in a Greek tragedy, where their futures were determined by the Fates setting the stage, leaving little to choice.

Overwrought by distress, the father of the two boys walked through the rest of his days like one already dead. Samuel's tender young spirit was deeply stricken when he saw his ailing father's condition. Once the apple of his father's eye, he was never able to shake the memory of his father's rage and bizarre existence.

⚬══⟩ ⟨══⚬

The lad's efforts to compensate for the wrong done to Jacob began early, and his demons gave him no rest. The once outgoing lad, who at one time made friends so easily, now lost them just as readily by being pensive and refusing to talk. He wandered aimlessly about the fields or stayed in the barn with the animals.

Young Samuel fought against the demons with bonehard labor. He put forth a constant effort to prove himself worthy of the "tainted" Blessing his father had inadvertly passed to him. He resented the fickle stepmother and felt the sting of rejection after she had turned the tables against him. He spent little time in the house, following all the signs of a mighty man of the field.

Meanwhile Jacob, badgered by his own set of demons, wondered whether he would ever to able to forgive his brother of such a transgression. He stayed under cover in the house, where the fickle stepmother doted on him like she once had doted upon Samuel.

With relationships so fractured and family loyalty so divided, the brothers spent little time together. They soon grew apart. Still, their spirits longed for the return of a commonality. Each depended upon the other to cut through the ice and bring their relationship where it longed to be.

⚬══⟩ ⟨══⚬

Meanwhile Samuel grew increasingly hard for his stepmother to deal with. He turned to his father and became the apple of his eye. The twin brothers drifted apart emotionally. They seldom bothered to speak to one another. But with "blood being thicker than water," a hidden loyalty kept resurfacing, first for one and then for the other, only to be suppressed by their stubborn constitutions.

Samuel suffered ups and downs from the emotional upheaval. When he was up, it was from feeling powerful with possessing the blessing of the fathers. When he was down, he was down on himself, wounded to the core for what he had done to his brother. Whether up or down, ever present in his mind was the hope of somehow turning back time and giving back what he had stolen from his brother Jacob.

He resolved to give back what he had taken once they reached the age of accountability, the age when the brothers were expected to exercise responsibility for their *blessing*.

⊷═◉ ◉═⊷

As the brothers approached the age of accountability, however, each one dealt with his issues in his individual way. Samuel, who was deeply sensitive and guilt-ridden, was driven by the desire to make things right and to be at peace with his brother. Jacob, on the other hand, nursed his resentment by stuffing it inside. For the sensitive Samuel -- who could read his brother's mind – this was for him the worst kind of rejection.

Before their age of accountability, Samuel and Jacob were made aware of the grave responsibility surrounding their generational blessing. However, after the scheming stepmother had tainted the sacred blessing, she peeled away the moral fiber from her stepsons, leaving them spiritually bankrupt and unable to deal with the responsibility. They remembered all too well their dying father's anger, but individual hurts stood in the way of making *anything* right.

Jacob, stoic and self-righteous like his father, would have forgiven his brother, but anger stood in his way and he wasn't able to let the anger go. He sought the guidance of the church elders to declare him the rightful heir to his father's blessing, but the elders would have nothing to do with such a controversy. No elder dared even *think* to interfere with God's hand!

At times Jacob wanted to overlook his brother's transgression, but he was stuck in the belief that the *Blessing* – though squandered through no fault of his own – remained a sin, a blasphemy against the Holy Ghost and a violation against an Almighty God. Many times Jacob thought that he had heard people say that his so called sin was an unpardonable abomination. He simply could not leave things alone.

⊷═◉ ◉═⊶

After the brothers reached adulthood, Jacob was ordained a preacher by lot, an onerous responsibility that left him all the more deprived of his father's blessing. All this only heaped all the more guilt and helplessness upon young Samuel. The family curse remained and Jacob continued to sulk.

Jacob, an angry man, was convinced that the condemnation he himself felt toward Samuel was the same way God felt about Samuel. Jacob did not set out to hate his brother Samuel, but he could not abandon the mindset that Samuel had blasphemed the Holy Ghost, committing an unpardonable act that could never be forgiven. The brothers were caught up in the constant heat of argument, followed by a silent anger and finally by a lifelong standoff.

The standoff was especially stressful for Jacob. Every day he woke up with a hole in his heart and did not know what was bringing him all the pain. In turn he rejected his twin brother Samuel by "shunning" him, a self-righteous act of the cruelest kind.

⊷═◉ ◉═⊶

Meanwhile, Samuel continued to want Jacob's acceptance in the worst way, but he went at it the wrong way. He often spoke harshly to his brother, driving him further away with threats made in anger, not gaining anyone any acceptance at all. Jacob finally shied away from the outspoken Samuel. In time neither of them was able to speak about *anything*.

In time Samuel lost all interest in this father's *Blessing*. He even turned against preserving the sanctity of the forefathers and owning the land and carrying forth the name. He no longer wished to forgive his brother, because without anger there would have been no "energy." Alas, the same anger that provided him with negative energy also shriveled his very soul.

Samuel was prone to heavy glooms that settled on him and slowed him down to where he had a hard time thinking of anything else. Day after day he worked himself out of his senses with hard labor. At night he was exhausted by his own moodiness. His personal hygiene suffered and his health waxed and waned, like the weather.

⊶⇒ ⇐⊷

Samuel had no regard for his fellowman and little regard for even himself, for that matter. He gradually slipped further and further into the lowlife. He found himself in frequent fights at the local *Biergarten*, believing that was the only way to cope with the constant stress.

He spent his evenings at local watering holes. Now and then, after hard labor by day and fighting at night, he did not make it back to where he lived while working as a hired hand. He sat disoriented by the side of the road, falling asleep waiting for someone to come along and direct him toward home.

When the constabulary came by, they arrested him for vagrancy or public drunkenness and put him into the local gulag to "sleep it off." This happened so often it that became a standing joke among the officers. Other times he fell asleep at the pub – at a table or on the floor – then turned himself in at the local gulag for the night.

After numerous overnight visits to and from the town gulag, nothing had improved. So the constabulary threw him into the local prison for a week. By the time Samuel was handed back to the peace officer, he would be well-rested and ended up going free, only to have the pattern repeat itself. Already Samuel Fisher was bringing upon himself the curse of his generation. After some time, he had begun to fool himelf to where he thought he actually *enjoyed* living the lowlife!

One officer finally grew so tired of the constant disrespect and growing pattern of verbal abuse, that he threw the young man into the penitentiary – lock, stock and barrel – to repent of his ways.

Samuel leaned into his cell wall and tried to sort things out. As child, he had been the apple of his father's eye, while Jacob lived in his brother's shadow. They both worked extremely hard. But no matter what they did, Samuel emerged the virtual leader, quietly and deliberatly elbowing himself in line for the leadership between the two brothers.

For so long the more passive Jacob had allowed his brother to inch his way forward that he no longer cared to be the leader. Things went as Samuel dictated as a matter of course, driving Jacob yet deeper into the background. Jacob was never outright jealous of Samuel. In fact he enjoyed being his brother's follower.

During their growing-up years, the brothers had scrapped about everything and could barely live in the same house. Samuel expressed his resentment by shooting venom at his brother by way of verbal abuse. Jacob, however, kept his resentment alive by "stuffing it in." He "expressed" himself by becoming *passive-aggressive.*

The brothers were seldom to speak together in a decent manner. In time their hatred deepened and poisoned their minds. First there had been the heat of argument, followed by the stress of silence, and finally by the constant strain of tension.

Over time there developed such a lifelong standoff that it ended up by placing the newest convict into the penitentiary for hating his brother. There the young man's anger only made him restless and did little to stir him to penitence. Matter of fact, the same anger and hatred that had separated young Samuel from the public had now followed him into the penitentiary.

◦━▷ ◁━◦

As Samuel leaned into the dirt wall, he was not about to repent of his ways. Individually the brothers had injured no one but themselves. After the tainting of their father's *Blessing,* Samuel thought he had to put up with his brother's passive aggressiveness. This caused him to become all the more angry with Jacob.

The anger seemed to work both ways. On the one hand, Jacob had never learned to forgive his brother either, and the wound would not heal. The longer the wound festered, the more it deviated between a downright personal hatred and all sorts of bitterness. One day, bitterness was all that Jacob had left. Every morning he woke up with the same festering sore and the same hole in his heart. And he did not know why.

Meanwhile Samuel was predestined to destruction by an extreme guilt he thought he had to carry around in a heavy black "backpack." By providence, he was helped from several unlikely but significant *Mentors.* First by a prison chaplain, then by an elderly Native American, and finally by a "brothel madam." No one could possibly conceive how that each of these extremely diverse and opposing characters and end up by impacting the same person!

Each one of the characters contained a story of his own. Each one brought his own separate and distinct drama into play as the circumstances enfolded, hence making each story enfold.

Thus was the plight of our hero, Pequea Sam.

Chapter 2

The Catacombs

The heavy iron and cement door grated and groaned heavily on its hinges, giving off a creaking sound that sent a grave message the entire long passageway with tombs and caves, reverberating into every corner. A grim reminder to Samuel about how he hated his brother and of what might be coming.

The purpose behind Samuel's incarceration in the first place was to separate him from the general public after he had been adjudged a menace to others and a threat to society. There the prisoner was expected to ponder the error of his way. Samuel did indeed ponder the error of his way.

"But I'm not about to repent of anything!"

His contentious spirit appeared to follow him everywhere. When his prison demeanor grew increasingly harsh, he grew to be hated by guards and fellow inmates alike. The unrepentant prisoner seemed to "like" living on the edge of violence.

The very worst anybody dared do was to *touch* a guard or officer. But the day Samuel jumped a guard in the midst a chow hall melee, placing his hands on "one of the prison's finest" he was banished to solitary confinement post-haste. to the dreaded "hole" a/k/a the *Catacombs*.

In Samuel's day, the "hole" was for those who liked flirting with death. The prisons were designed to be brutal enough to turn any convict "inside out." To be declared non-correctable was a hard enough thing. But to be thrown into the Catacombs with the worst of *thugs,* was a bitter pill for even the most incorrigible to swallow. For the first time young Samuel feared for his life!

⟊⟐ ⟐⟊

The Catacombs, patterned after those from ancient Rome, consisted of an underground cemetery composed of galleries, or passages, with side recesses to handle tombs. The penitentiary, or main prison, was generally located some three miles outside of a town's limits. The main pen was customarily constructed right on the top of the Catacombs.

Because of their intricate layout and access to open country via secret passageways, the prison Catacombs were often used as hiding places for potential victims in times of persecution and civil commotion.

⟊⟐ ⟐⟊

Samuel's new "quarters" were connected to just such an underground passageway, with recesses dug into walls for tombs and human remains and the like. Needless to reiterate, the Catacombs were by far the most dreaded of an entire prison system. There the incorrigible would be sentenced to spend his natural life in prison time by himself.

Young Samuel's "grave-like cell" was situated within a series of "hives" that contained individual "tombs." Each *tomb,* measured roughly six feet long and six feet wide, with barely enough room to stand up.

Behind a small door, a tiny table was bolted to the wall. In the center of the table was an indentation, or *crucible,* into which the guard poured water for drinking and washing via an opening in the door called a *cubby-hole*. Through the same cubby hole the guard shoved the prisoner's food, meager portions of stale bread.

Secured to another wall was a bucket into which the inmate was expected to do *his business*. The only thing better than being in a grave itself was that in this one the prisoner was still breathing!

◆━○ ○━◆

The new convict, sentenced to the Catacombs, alone and forlorn, lies on his threadbare mat and stares into the ceiling of his sepulchre-like cell. He shares his mat with flies and bugs and waits out the lonely death of the unrepentant. Young Samuel begins to feel the curse of his generation as tries to muster up some sort of "bravery." Yet the slam of the iron and concrete door sounds so violent and feels so final, young Samuel wonders if he will ever again see the light of day.

"Gotta live in a cell no bigger than a shoe box, but by gosh I'm tough enough to handle almost anything!"

The newest of the prisoners had not yet settled after the futile altercation with one of the prison's finest. And he was surely not ready to give up the aggressive behavior that got him into the penitentiary in the first place. He lays quietly and listens to the haunting stillness as up and down the endless hives his fellow inmates stir restlessly on their meager dirt floors and wait for the morning. He listens to the moans of those who seek escape through starvation, or of those who refuse the back-breaking labor on the prison farm. Now and then he hears a pained out-of-body groan and realizes it's his own.

Needless to mention, Samuel did not do well his first night inside his tomb. He spent the painfully long hours boxed into the heavy blackness of a cave, sleeping fitfully at best.

"There will be a way. They can't more'n kill me, can they!"

⋯⟹ ⟸⋯

Midway through the first morning, the voice of authority called through the cubby-hole in the door. "I'm here to talk to you!"

"Imagine that! Well, go away, you! I have no time for the likes of you!" The "visitor" did not belabor the issue lest he infuriate the reluctant inmate all the more. Samuel rolled over on his belly and went back to sleep. He felt no regret over the way he had just blown off yet another "voice of authority."

Eventually Samuel maintained a bitter standoff with *anyone* in authority. When the guard on duty threw the day's portion of bread and water into his crucible, he had already decided to refuse to take any rations. *"Nothing like getting this over with soon as possible. One way or another."*

Sometime during the same afternoon, a counselor spoke through the cubby hole. However, Samuel had already decided he had no time for the counselor and did not even bother to talk to him.

For a long while, young Samuel lay on the dirt mat, hands behind his head, thinking the confusing thoughts of the newly incarcerated. *"Ignore them and they'll go away. Same with their rotten chow!"*

Both the chaplain and the counselor, *would-be rescuers,* were conditioned not to give up so readily on the young man. The following morning the same voice was at the cubby-hole. "Something for you," said the now vaguely familiar voice. Samuel rolled off of his mat and picked up the object the voice had just tossed onto his grub table. He rolled it around in his hands and peered at it in the semi-darkness. "Book of Psalms?"

"Not in the mother tongue!" In a feigned self-righteous manner, still acting tough, the prisoner tossed the book in the direction of

the business bucket and slithered back across the floor. *"That's as low as it gonna get, I reckon."*

Morning followed another night of fitful sleep for the young prisoner. Toxic anger occupied his mind by day, and the pangs of hunger kept him awake by night. Day after day the same thing.

He ate less and less, sleeping the sleep of starvation, as the standoff continued. The counselor, who had long decided the prisoner was crazy to begin with, had been avoiding him, satisfied that he was not going to be responsible for such a silent, angry kid. The hunger strike continued to the point where "the silent, angry kid" became emaciated and non-responsive.

Chaplain Visser, however, saw in the kid something worth saving. *"Love sticks closer than a brother!"* Driven by the mantra, he stuck by Samuel like a faithful servant, hoping for the *Beauty of Kindness* to raise the young convict above his barbarism. *Like a rose lifting its head from the desert floor.*

Every day Chaplain Visser returned to the tomb to try to get his prisoner to talk. "Just a little something?" But every day the young man stayed locked in the prison of the mind, thinking he had to reap for his transgression against his family into his third and fourth generation. Day after day he told Chaplain Visser, *"Get lost, I tell you! Leave me alone already!"*

⊷══◉ ◉══⊷

Eventually the young prisoner's voice was barely audible from non-use. The day he did not respond at all – not even to tell Weaver to get lost – turned into an extremely anxious day for the chaplain. He leaned his head against the concrete door and uttered a prayer of desperation for the young prisoner put to his charge, then started down the dark corridor in deep angst, fearing the young man was not going to be alright.

One last time the chaplain turned back and peered through the cubby-hole. "Talk to me; just one word to tell me you're okay." The chaplain, speaking into the darkness, was greeted with the long, throaty moan of a dying man.

The rapid pounding of the guard's oversized boots echoed up and down the corridor on the way back from summoning help. The concrete door groaned under its own weight, and for first time the chaplain was able to see inside the cell. Mice had worked over the mold-covered bread on the crucible inside the door. The smell of death permeated the tomb-like cell. A lone prisoner lay on the floor, curled up like a fetus.

The jailer dragged the emaciated prisoner across the dirt floor and dumped him at the cell door. "Look like he's been tryin' to die. Looks like he'll likely git 'er done, regardless of what we try to do about it," said the guard, walking through the cell door.

"And you were gonna let it happen? Just like that?"

"What'cha expect *me* to do about it!"

"Well, you better do somethin' better'n just stand there!"

"Look, he's already in the grave," chuckled the hardened jailer to justify his inaction.

"So bring him forth!" The angry chaplain demanded, sounding like the Master when He ordered the gravekeeper to set his friend Lasarus free.

"All yours; have at it," the jailer shrugged.

Chaplain Visser placed his hands across Samuel's breast and prayed for the Spirit to enter the dehydrated body. No response. He knelt by the lifeless body and tried it again.

Water gurgled down the prisoner's hatch and he coughed it back up. Several tries later, he took the water. With that, the good chaplain ran from the cell in search of something better than the stale bread. He made off a crock of soup from the Officers' Dining Quarters.

Back in the cell, Chaplain Visser immersed the stale bread into the crock of soup, then dropped the soggy wad down the starving man's gullet, like a mother bird nourishing her young. A few chunks was all the shrunken gut could contain.

All morning the "Good Samaritan" force-fed the starving prisoner, one soggy wad at a time. Now and then he placed his hands across the emaciated chest, hoping for the some warmth to enter. Just as the water had trumped the intense dehydration, so the soggy wads of moldy bread began to replace the deathlike gray in his cheeks with a slow, dramatic *pinkness*.

Throughout the next several days Chaplain Visser managed to get several wads down into the starving gullet. It must have felt good going down, because in a matter of days Samuel began to eat and drink on his own.

"I just might make it after all. Goodness knows, I'm orney enough!"

⊷═◓ ◔═⊶

One night Samuel feared he was going to die from the hunger strike. All night he travailed with the likelihood and wrestled with a very real fear. Early the next morning, when a surprised "Samaritan" approached the cubby-hole, the prisoner was already standing inside waiting for him. *"Think I could have something to read?"* Nothing was said about the book he had tossed at the business bucket.

Chaplain Visser, whose habit it was to carry a leather-bound book of parables called *Gospel of John* under his arm, reached through the hole and placed the book into the eager young man's outstretched hands.

Alas, Samuel found to his astonishment that after many days without natural light, his eyesight had gone south. Along with the distraction of constant hunger pangs, his voice had become barely audible. He could not see to read the book the chaplain had handed him, but he loved the feel of leather in his fingers.

"I promise not to trash this one!"

The feel of the leather-bound book Chaplain Visser had placed into the prisoner's hands, captivated him as he waited for another visit from the chaplain. *"Would you read some of this to me?"*

Jesus the Master often spoke in parables. "A parable is an *earthly* story with a *heavenly* meaning," the chaplain instructed. Day after day the chaplain delivered the Master's parables to eager young ears just inside the cubby-hole. His mind was still sharp from its long fasting stage. He gripped every word like a vise, containing every word the faithful chaplain read to him.

Samuel had honed his memory skills through the art of listening, and listening all he had. He quickly developed a knack for converting a story into rote memory. In a matter of days the parables in the *Gospel of John,* read to Sam and repeated to himself throughout the night, began to take on "power."

The leftover pangs of starvation had all but lifted from the prisoner's emaciated body. He began to make out shapes in the semi-darkness. Eager hands held onto the leather-bound book, rolling it around in shaky fingers.

Reading the Scripture in other than the German, native tongue and language of the Church, had been *verboten* during Samuel's growing up years. That had likely conditioned the way he treated the first book that Chaplain Weaver had placed through the cubby-hole, the one that had ended up in the *business bucket.*

For the first time, Samuel would forgo the demands of a self-righteous father and allow the chaplain to read in a language he understood clearly. At night his eager mind played back the "memory tapes" that earlier had issued from the faithful chaplain's lips.

Samuel became more and more eager to read for himself. Lo his young and supple eyes had improved throughout the time his body remained in a fasting state. Still with the hampered eyesight, the process was long and slow.

"Think I could have another Book of Psalms?"

"Every Psalm is a song to be sung, a prayer to be prayed," the faithful chaplain expounded, surprised that Samuel remembered throwing the first book into the *business bucket* some weeks earlier.

Enhanced by the fasting state, Samuel's mind gripped every word like a vise. He clung to every psalm as he squinted to read, reading the same lines over and over until they stuck indelibly in his hungered mind. He memorized with a vengeance. In the dead of night he repeated aloud what the heart and gut had contained throughout the day.

With Chaplain Visser as a constant sounding board, the young man's voice, stilled by half-death and extended periods of non-use, grew stronger until he was finally able to articulate. With that Samuel recited aloud the verses he had mastered in the black of night. Every morning he spoke a verse or two to the chaplain – one time a song, another time a prayer.

⊶══◉ ◉══⊷

"Not on your life. That kid is deranged. Hard as a steel trap." The warden was not about to release Samuel from the security of his "grave" and place him back into prison population. Day after day Chaplain Visser crusaded to get Samuel out of the Catacombs. Despite the Warden's determined stance, Chaplain Visser stayed patient and believed for a breakthrough.

The Commonwealth had been considering banging Samuel with another assault charge stemming from a laundry list of former charges. If that were the case, he would leave administrative custody (the hole) to be bound over for trial and the sentencing on the newest charges.

"Justice must be served, after all," said the higher powers. "Freedom is not ready and cheap, for this one especially. As far as I'm concerned, he can stay in the Catacombs 'til he rots! Only right for putting his filthy hands all over one the finest of my men!"

In time, and with the persuasion of Chaplain Visser and a few of his fellow "crusaders", young Samuel was given the option of serving additional time in the hole in exchange for dropping the new charges. *The long arm of the law reaching forth and at the same time pulling back?*

Even in his tomb-like cell, Samuel seldom felt forsaken, often too excited even to eat or sleep. He listened while his prayers pierced the outer blackness of the night. Samuel preferred to remain where he was.

"The Catacombs are becoming a personal 'monastery'!"

⊷⟞⟝ ⟞⟝⟝⊶

"The young man is worth redeeming," said the chaplain.

"How would you know?"

"It's certainly worth trying. Let me have him, if only during a few hours at the end of my duty," Visser pleaded.

"It's them filthly opiates," mumbled the deputy warden, suspecting that the young prisoner and his chaplain might be up to something.

Chaplain Visser was relentless, both in his endeavor to see Samuel get well from the effects of his near starvation, as well as in his pursuit of his asylum. First thing every morning the faithful chaplain visited Samuel's tomb-like cell to persuade him to get off his mat and to say something, *anything*, through his cubby-hole.

The chaplain's undying interest in his young prisoner caught the attention of the constabulary. Before long it had piqued the interest of all others in authority, enough to become a matter for them to check out. "Let me join you next time you talk to the kid," suggested the captain of the jailers.

The prisoner's eyes had not enjoyed natural light since he left the prison population for the dimly lit Catacombs. He could barely make out the shape of the "talking hole," but well enough to sense the direction of sound from the outside and from the meager light coming in through the cubby-hole. He been forced to "see" by way of his other senses.

Once at the hole, he was barely able to distinguish the outline of the chaplain's features from a foot away. Then could only whisper through the hole. What was once meant to be "spiritual refreshment" from Chaplain Visser, had become a critical exercise in perception for the young prisoner. Both men knew the absolute value in going through this meager exercise in perception, sometimes several times a day if the chaplain could swing it.

⊷⟫ ⟪⊶

The prison captain undid the heavy door. Light flooded the grave. Samuel cringed into the farthest corner, startled by the abrupt light. He responded sensibly, albeit in a whisper, during the captain's interview.

The captain found Samuel cooperative and articulate, even a bit convincing. But without his native "see chaplain" he was far from "spiritually refreshing." That did not surprise Chaplain Visser, however, who believed that such discernment should be reserved for the mouth of babes, not for the likes of those in the captain's world.

"I cannot release this kid over into your custody," declared the captain, walking back up the corridor. "What good is the prisoner to you anyhow, emaciated like some dead man, mute as a lump, barely able to see his hand in front of his face?"

Chaplain Visser did not know how to respond.

⊷⟹ ⟸⊶

The chaplain had started out assigned to work within the prison population. However, when his work with the young Samuel Fisher became such a daily activity, the prison captain provided the chaplain with a makeshift "office" just inside the entrance to the Catacombs.

Once again Chaplain Visser stood on the prison captain's carpet. "Tell you what we're gonna do. Once a day you can enter the kid's tomb to work with him up close and personal. Sooner you in the crazy kid's cell than him tailing you in population. Every day you will visit his cell and report back to me. Hear me. I said *every day!* Begin in twenty-four hours."

By the time the prison captain and his jailer met with Visser outside Samuel's tomb, it had been a painfully long twenty-four hours of anticipation. Chaplain Visser was anxious about what he might find after days of whispering through a hole and peering into the darkness. It was an emotional moment, hearing the mammoth stone door groaning in place and then grating against its rusted hinges.

Chaplain Visser did not know what to expect when the captain opened up the cell. Moving indeed, to so suddenly be close enough to touch the once-violent prisoner without the security of the heavy stone door.

Light from the corridor poured over the cobwebs and stench of a tomb not accustomed to the abruptness of natural light and air. A solitary path had worn its way from the dirt mat to the cubby-hole, the only route a virtually blind person would know to follow and the only part not strewn with moldy bread and contaminated with rodents.

The prisoner lumbered onto his elbow and peered at the silhouette piercing the semi-darkness. "I've come to commune with you," said the chaplain, his voice shaking. "I'm comin' in!"

"Imagine that," was all Samuel could utter, barely above a whisper, as Chaplain Visser boldly stepped into the sepulchre.

"Now we're both on the same side of the wall!" said Visser.

The prisoner pretended to be taken aback. *"We are now, ain't we!"*

Chaplain Visser was at a loss for words over what he found in the cell. "Like I said, I've come to commune with you, Samuel. One-on-one!" repeated the over-wrought chaplain.

"Yeah, really! Why don't you just go away and leave me be! Can't see, nohow!"

The prisoner really did not want to see *anybody* after he had gotten so comfortable "living in a dying mode." In barely audible terms he protested fiercely, cringing at the two figures as they cowered over him. The "figures" watched in silent awe as the prisoner regressed into his normal fetal position.

The prison captain, aghast at the squalor he had just found inside the sepulchre, changed his mind about allowing Chaplain Visser inside Samuel's cell. He sent his flunky down the corridor for two chairs and placed them outside the cell.

"Here ya have it. I'm givin' you have one hour a day with your prisoner, provided you spend it out *here*," he said, pointing at the two chairs, thereby revoking the warden's former offer.

⇥⟾ ⟸⇤

Working patiently day after day in the corridor outside of Samuel's tomb slowly bore its fruit. The inmate's pangs of starvation subsided and his health improved. Eventually he was able to retain a sense of joy in spite of what he had to endure inside the Catacombs. Samuel was gradually becoming resilient in his ability just to *survive*.

Alas, like one with a cleanly-swept house, his demons returned, each time accompanied by several new cronies to tempt Samuel. Depression set in. Anger resurfaced, along with a type of remorse over not being able to conquer the demons.

Hope, however, arrived with the morning. Every day at the crack of dawn, the creaking of the unoiled door into the corridor signaled the approach of the faithful chaplain. Often Samuel was already waiting for him just inside the peephole in his door.

After several days Samuel appeared more comfortable leaving his tomb for his daily visit with Chaplain Visser in the corridor. With that the warden increased the visiting times from one hour to two a day, one in the morning and one in the afternoon. After several weeks the once-reluctant inmate was given complete asylum with the chaplain. Following that the Warden moved Samuel's "new cell" next to Chaplain Visser makeshift office, a leap above the former "sepulchre." But it was still the dreaded Catacombs.

With each visit young Samuel grew more comfortable with his new surroundings and with his chaplain's visits. Slowly and reluctantly he began to open up to the chaplain – a few words at at time – about how he and his stepmother had misappropriated the "*blessing of the forefathers*" and about how the *Blessing* had been squandered.

It soon became clear to Chaplain Visser that Samuel carried a load of guilt over how things had gone down. Moreover, Samuel remained convinced that he had to shoulder the generational curse he believed was to come with the squandering of the *Blessing*.

Worse than anything was the guilt he felt from hating his stepmother. The chaplain tried to empathize with young Samuel, but the situation was so far removed from what he had ever experienced with his own mother, that he that he did not know how.

"Write a letter to your stepmother."

"No way! My stepmother is dead."

"Write her anyway."

"No. I hate her."

"Tell her so. Tell her how much you hate her."

"You gotta be plomb crazy, Man! I won't do such a thing! I can't, cause no matter how I hate her, she was still my mother!"

"Just do it. Your stepmother is dead already. Besides, it's not like you're sending something to HER!"

All night Samuel scribbled freely in the darkness, spilling his guts and shooting venom at his stepmother to the point of exhaustion.

"Now, tear it up and write her again!"

The next morning, a weary youth waved a handful of loose papers at the chaplain. *"I already did, see?"*

"Now then, write her and tell her you forgive her."

"That I will NOT do! End of discussion!"

"Just for me, Samuel?"

It was an agonizing chore for the young convict, feeling the gnawing of unforgiveness he'd been suppressing over the years. Nevertheless he fought the pain and put his shoulder to the task.

When Chaplain Visser came by to check on Samuel's progress, he waved the "forgiveness letter" at him – *all three words of it.*

The chaplain spoke without hesitation. "Now write your father."

Samuel expected as much. He was ready.

Samuel's exercise in forgiveness with his parents was over. Now he wanted nothing more than to have things be right with his brother. Emotionally spent, in the quiet of night, he volunteered his own letter to Jacob.

He got nowhere for pondering whether Jacob would even answer a letter if he *did* get one together. *"This one would be the hardest of all, even if I could do it!"* In his vacillation, Samuel's resentment toward Jacob resurfaced. All night he went "through it" with his estranged brother.

Samuel had so successfully "passed" Chaplain Visser's "letters test" that the chaplain was moved to ask the warden to let his convict be outside the Catacombs. Young Samuel felt game and adventurous, but still the stable of demons clamored to occupy his cleanly-swept house. All night, he battled the demons tooth and nail with little rest. By morning the warfare against the enemy of his soul waned, leaving him preoccupied and physically weak.

Despite becoming a model prisoner, Samuel remained banished to the Catacombs for his earlier aggression against an officer out in population. But though virtually blind, whenever he was called upon to be useful up and down the corridor, he was pleased to do it. No matter what the chore, Samuel performed it responsibly and with quiet pleasure.

⊷⊐ ⊏⊶

The return of Samuel's outward physical health brought with it an *inner* change as well. He started out by thinking new thoughts, and the change was swift and complete, rendering him a changed man, ever excited about the newly-found prison savvy and about tackling each new day with his faithful chaplain.

Samuel, anticipating to be released back to population, resolved in his heart to better himself right where he was. *"I'll bloom where I'm planted! Every remaining day in this corridor of tombs, I shall make a noble effort to make me a new friend and find at least one fellow inmate in need."*

Gradually the young prisoner's charisma reached into the fractured spirit of even the hardest inmate, so that over time the pleasant demeanor softened a few hardened hearts inside the Catacombs. The rowdy ones became less boisterous and there was less cursing up and down the corridor.

On a good day, the "hole" population appeared less incorrigible than even the general prison population. Guards and officers who had earlier refused hole duty began asking to work their beats inside the hostile Catacombs.

As the changing young man developed his people skills, long since hidden, he also uncovered a lot of prison savvy. In time he gradually earned favor with his jailers. Chaplain Visser seized upon this opportunity to have young Samuel released from the Catacombs.

That was not going to happen, but it did lead to a compromise between the chaplain and his constabulary. Samuel could spend supervised time outside his tomb, on condition that he spend it in the corridor area directly outside his tomb, at all times accompanied by Chaplain Visser.

The young convict, however, was content just to stay in the safe and predictable confines of his hive of tombs. In fact he was reluctant to leave his area at all, horrified by things being so free and open. He was far from ready to rely on his failing eyesight without clinging onto Visser. However, over time the youthful prisoner was game and he relented. Visser began walking his charge outside his tomb to determine whether he could stand on two legs and get one foot to follow the other.

Getting out of the tomb-like cell was the greatest possible breakthrough for Samuel, who now found a way to exercise his limbs. It was a breakthrough for the chaplain as well, who was now able to spend quality time with the young charge. Up close and personal, if only for a minutes each day.

A few minutes outside the tomb worked wonders for Samuel from the very first day. He became highly motivated to becoming well and strong. Night after night he practiced walking in his "tomb," sliding along the walls and holding on as best he could. *"Some day I am going to up and walk outside this rotten tomb, all my own myself, without the help of even my "seeing-eye dog!"*

Every day the faithful chaplain reported Samuel's progress outside of the tomb to his supervisor. The constabulary became so impressed with the progress that he ordered that they could walk up and down the corridor directly outside of Samuel's hive. If that went well, they could eventually earn some "yard-time."

"I am far from ready for that!"

As the two conditioned their thinking toward yard time, Chaplain Visser was elated. However, his young prisoner remained apprehensive because he thought he could not see. *"Main thing, I would be scared to death by just the SOUND of all those voices outside of the main prison population!"*

"Time to bite the bullet," announced Chaplain Visser as the two made their way toward a secret passage at the outermost end of the Catacombs. The seldom used passage, formerly the avenue of escape during persecution or civil commotion, now led into the exercise yard for *yard-out*. Visser's reluctant prisoner was finally biting the bullet, at least to see if he could manage one footstep behind the other.

Once through the passage, Samuel had to trust his feet to make it through the uneven gravel. Furthermore, he had to trust Chaplain Visser to be his eyes. He dared not make the slightest move without the chaplain. His failing eyesight left him vulnerable as they faced the glaring sunlight; still more as the two approached the exercise yard with all the chatter in the prison yard.

"That's it!" he said in something between a managed whisper and a groan after a single round around the cinder track. *"Simply too petered!"*

The two sat on the wall right outside the weight pit. Samuel was hopelessly disoriented by the clanging of barbells and the chatter of inmate talk down inside the weight pit. Needless to say, the first day at yard-out turned out to be a shambles. *"I will NOT go out THERE again!"*

Samuel had anticipated seeing some of his fellow inmates from the general population when he got out to the yard. But he was too busy figuring out exactly just where they were and preoccupied with sticking close to his *seeing-eye dog* and not letting his sense get in the way of what they were going.

⊷⇒ ⇐⊷

On another yard-out, perhaps a week later, Visser came to bring Samuel with him and get him to starting to exercise. *"I am inclined to stay in the safety of my tomb in the Catacombs!"*

The young prisoner finally agreed to go. However, he refused to do anything without Visser's reassuring touch or the sound of his voice right beside him. The two sat on a concrete bench outside the weight pit. After a few minutes Samuel asked to be taken back to his tomb, where he would again be familiar and safe.

Another week later, with the daily fresh air and warm sunshine, the two left the secret passage out of the Catacombs. *"Ya know I am actually starting to trust the feel the gravel under my feet!"*

At all times, Samuel perceived the reassuring presence of his mentor walking beside him. He not only trusted the gravel under his feet, but he began to trust the healing in his eyes from the sunshine. Enough to see the image of his mentor and the shape of a solitary evergreen off in a nearby copse of other trees. *Cause for celebration!*

The following week at yard-out, Visser noticed that Samuel walked with his eyes lowered. *"I look down at my feet because I am marching to the rhythm of my own mantra."*

"Look forward and upward! Try not to look at your feet this entire lap."

After several days of habitually *looking forward and upward,* the prisoner's confidence gradually arose. As though by some miracle, he identified the familiar outline of a hill off in the horizon. Before the week's end, Samuel's faith had increased to where he was able to distinguish the outline of the larger trees in the horizon, albeit barely.

⊷⊐◯ ◯⊏⊶

"What are you feeling about your brother nowadays?" Chaplain Visser casually asked his prisoner.

Samuel glared at Visser's question. Resentment resurfaced and for days young Samuel went "through it" with his chaplain.

"You've been murmuring a lot lately," suggested Chaplain Visser during a subsequent yard-out. "What's up with that?"

Samuel answered before Visser's words were barely out. *"I murmur about my brother all the time!"*

The prompt answer startled Visser, who for the first time heard Samuel utter a single word about his estranged brother. Chaplain Visser rejoiced in the breakthrough. However the elation was short-lived, coming at the heels of yet another of Samuel's awful downers.

⊷⊐◯ ◯⊏⊶

At the sound of his own words, Samuel's anger toward Jacob was suddenly renewed. Once more his demons fought to occupy his cleanly-swept house, like a swarm of locusts ready to devour what had become so good for the young man who'd begun to slowly turn inside out.

"Why the mischief doesn't my brother Jacob honor the Blessing I received from my father?" murmured the angry young man, ending the subject as quickly as the chaplain had tried bringing it up.

⟶ ⟵

"The spirit is heavy again today," observed Chaplain Visser.

"Yes, Guru; heavy indeed; and getting heavier all the time!"

"Let's we talk about it."

"I think all the time of my brother out there somewhere, how he dishonors me and is envious because I have the so-called Blessing of the Forefathers. How can I carry out the spiritual responsibility when his injurious spirit stands in the way?"

"Look at it this way. You can't *make* your brother forgive you, not any more than you can get him to stop dishonoring you. Love him anyway and free yourself from this web of anger. However, first you gotta forgive *yourself* for deceiving *him*. Only then can you forgive him for dishonoring you. Walk a day in his shoes and accept him for what he is. Then kill him with kindness. End of lecture."

"I didn't need your lecture!"

"Look at yourself, Pal. You've just passed through the valley of the shadow of death. *You yourself* have been lifted from the pit of destruction. Your feet have been planted on a rock. It stands to reason that you should in turn forgive *your* fellowman."

All night Samuel pondered his chaplain's "lecture." He wrestled with his angel to be freed from the prison of his own mind, from hating his brother. Into the wee hours he pondered whether he could do what needed to be done, without anger and resentment standing in the way.

Samuel's demeanor changed at the prospect of forgiving his brother and expecting nothing in return. At once he felt released from the prison of his own mind. Set free! In turn he freed Jacob to be who he was meant to be, without his anger standing in the way. Samuel's whole being took the words to heart. So seriously did he take the resolve that it changed the very way he thought and spoke. He started by forgiving himself, then forgiving everything and everybody else.

Chapter 3

Billy Penn

Meanwhile William Penn a/k/a Billy Penn, young Quaker missionary, sought converts to settle in the New World as part of what he called his "Holy Experiment."

Chaplain Visser learned of Billy Penn's missionary endeavors and sent word for him to come to the penitentiary and interview a "young Samuel Fisher" as a potential candidate.

The Prison Warden agreed to allow Penn to come inside the confines of the penitentiary to interview a candidate, provided the inmate being interviewed had proven himself to be sufficiently penitent.

Stories about the young Amish inmate had been spreading up and down the Catacombs. When the stories began leaking from the Catacombs up to the main prison population, the constabulary paid close heed to the stories and found young Samuel Fisher to be without guile.

⋆⟫⟦ ⟧⟪⋆

"Your best prospect is a young Amish man exiled to the Catacombs," said Chaplain Visser in his first meeting with Billy Penn. "There's virtually no missionary potential anywhere else in this prison's huge population."

Samuel, I'd like to talk with you about a young missionary from the New World. His name is William Penn, 'Billy for short'," announced Chaplain Visser, after broaching the subject to his young charge.

The chaplain began first by appealing for an interview to the Warden, who protested vehemently about bringing Samuel up from the Catacombs just for *some interview*. The Warden changed his mind and later relented and opened the way for Penn.

"Why would I want to talk to anybody, and to some missionary, of all people! Get serious, Guru!"

"I want you to talk to the missionary about going to the New World."

"Get serious, Guru. Why would I even wanna go to the New World? My place is right here."

"You could begin a new life there, across the Water."

"My place is right here, making things right with my brother Jacob."

"Your brother wants nothing to do with you, Samuel. I can't as much as get him to visit you in prison."

"Jacob has forgiven me. He sees no need to visit me, and I agree!"

"He forgives you with his lips but not in his heart."

"But he's a preacher. Why would a preacher not forgive from his heart?"

"Because he may not know how. He may very well have forgiven you, but then he goes back and dwells on your transgression against him, that how it's an abomination in the eyes of God."

"Does Jacob *know* I forgive him from the heart?"

"Sure he knows it. He's says he's done the same thing for you, that he's done all he can do."

"Then he's written me off as a lost cause?"

"No more than you did to him, 'til just recently."

"I need to talk to him."

"Forget about him. Leave your brother alone."

Samuel leaned into the wall and hung his head. That's all he *could* do.

⊹⟫⟪⊹

Life for Samuel, albeit still in the Catacombs, moved forward so long as he had Chaplain Visser to confide in and the Holy Spirit to comfort him. Nonetheless, life for the young prisoner was a constant quandary. Every day he seemed to face another new trial now that he enjoyed better health.

Every day Samuel pondered the prospect of going to the New World. At night he struggled with the relationship between him and Jacob, afraid his brother's unforgiving spirit was going to trip him up.

One the one hand, going to the New World has been affording Samuel a new start, a different vision to follow. On the other hand, it was forever separating him from his closest flesh and blood, frustrating any hope of reconciling with Jacob, or whether Jacob had in fact even forgiven him.

Remaining in the Old Country offered hope for reconciliation. But it also meant continued exile in the Catacombs. Young Samuel struggled with his options, a cup he wished could pass from him. For now, life in the Catacombs would continue, the place where he had already learned to be content with the way it was.

Chaplain Visser's afternoons had again been relegated to the general prison population, but the faithful servant still found time to spend yard time with his convict. There the sunlight and fresh air prospered Samuel in health as well as in spirit.

Every day brought new challenges for Samuel. He raised the hackles of the prison constabulary and jeopardized the chaplain's position when they learned he was sending letters of remorse and forgiveness to Jacob. Never did Jacob as much as acknowledge any expression of remorse or any plea for forgiveness. Still Samuel's forgiveness – unilateral and unconditional – remained extended to his brother.

✤══ ══✤

The Prison Superintendent had formerly informed Chaplain Visser that Penn had been seeking models for his "Holy Experiment." "Who would be a better model for the Experiment than young Samuel Fisher?" Chaplain Visser was quick to reply. But all that to no avail.

On occasion Chaplain Visser returned to Samuel with the latest about Billy Penn and his much-talked about "Holy Experiment." Conditioned by his Old Order Amish teaching, Samuel's mind remained closed to any idea about missionaries in general. Much less moving to the New World. *My mission is right here, Guru, up and and down these Catacombs!*

Samuel hoped that one day the Warden would find it in heart to give him free rein to spread some "spiritual refreshment" up and down the corridors. Samuel pondered his uncertain future.

✤══ ══✤

One day the Master did indeed tilt His hand. "Could you get me time with the warden so that I might speak with him about a young convict confined to the Catacombs?" asked Billy Penn. "From what I've been hearing, this is quite an extraordinary young fellow. Perhaps he could help us set the stage for others to come and settle in the New World. Who knows?"

Chaplain Visser lost no time in approaching the warden for young Penn. "In lieu of serving out his sentence here in the Old

Country, I respectfully request you 'exile' him to the New World as part of Penn's 'Experiment'."

"I will consider allowing the young Quaker inside the prison for an interview or so, but I forbid him talking to anyone in the Catacombs, much less recommending a'body for asylum in the New World," the Warden mandated.

Billy Penn took the Warden's position as a flat-out "no." But Chaplain Visser, with persuasive power and the benefit of good administrative rapport, resolved to turn to the Warden's position into a yes.

The Deputy Warden, flanked by two guards, took Samuel from the Catacombs. They shackled the surprised young convict hand and foot and led him through the main prison population. He had no idea where they were leading him until he sat face to face with Billy Penn inside the Warden's office.

"I hear all these good reports about you," Billy said.

"I try to do the right thing."

"You come highly recommended. I want you to consider being part of my 'Holy Experiment'."

"Why me?"

"Because the warden and chaplain have both decided that you would be an excellent candidate to take in the Experiment. Would you consider locating to the New World?"

"No, I will stay in my own country. My work is right here; right in these Catacombs!" Samuel did not mince words and did not elaborate.

There were more meetings in the warden's office. Each meeting concluded with one more reason why the reluctant youth would keep saying no to Penn's Experiment. First it was the obvious: *"I do not want to give up my Amish faith for Billy Penn's Quakerism."*

"We will concede that. You don't have to give up *anything*."

"What about the time I have yet to serve in this place?"

"Billy will see about a Governor's pardon."

"But I don't want to be so far away from my brother."

Samuel's hope for reconciliation with his brother was more compelling than any hoped-for release. Each time any Warden they approached him, the matter was let go for another time. Meanwhile, Samuel continued his good image in the eyes of the warden and the Prison Superintendent.

"The warden will give you time on your own to go up and down the corridor for an hour every day to talk to fellow inmates in the Catacombs,"

Visser informed Samuel one day, out of the blue. The elated young convict was now all the more convinced that he was right where he belonged, that he could continue to bloom where God had planted him. Talking to his friends through their cubby-holes had been a specific answer to specific prayer.

As time wore on, Samuel got to spend more and more time outside the confines of his designated "grave." One day he found himself without supervision at all, spending time in his "tomb" only to be alone.

"You will locate to population and share space with me up there," said Chaplain Visser, whose office had long since been moved upstairs from the Catacombs to work with the other inmates in the general prison population.

"How's come, Guru?"

"It's about proving yourself trustworthy."

The warden's deputy informed Samuel that he had now been given free rein within the general prison population and in the Catacombs as well. After he was entrusted not to lock up except at night, Samuel was convinced that God's hand was moving the Warden.

That no concession was made in Samuel's sentence was of no concern to him, so confident was he about blooming where he was planted, albeit in the Catacombs of some way-out prison.

Samuel's chief concern remained for the burden he carried for his estranged brother, from whom he had heard nothing despite numerous pleas for forgiveness and hoped-for reconciliation.

Chaplain Visser gave his argument one final thrust before throwing in towel. "Making such a big change during this stage in your life would be pretty scary, I know. But know what would be even scarier? *Regret!*"

In time Samuel wearied of saying no to Chaplain Visser and Billy Penn. He began giving serious thought to the New World. *"I much prefer to stay where I am, working on making things right with my brother. On the other hand, if he and I are not able to connect while I'm locked up in here, what's the difference if I continue trying it from the New World?"*

⊷═◌ ◌═⊷

William Penn Jr. (Billy) was born in London in 1644. Early on he gave up a promising medical career to pursue his ongoing radical beliefs. Billy had converted to the Quaker faith in his early twenties. After he converted to Quakerism, he was filled with religious fervor and missionary zeal.

Young Billy had made missionary journeys from his native England to Holland and Germany. His mission was to establish a place where he and those who were like-minded would be able to experience and to practice their "Quaker" concepts.

⊷═◌ ◌═⊷

Billy Penn's inexhaustible energy propelled him ahead of his time. His was a lively voice and a most effective instrument in a largely illiterate population. First it was the Catholics in Europe, and then in America it was the English. Eventually Penn's radical faith and substantial wealth, coupled with his aristocratic connections, made Pennsylvania possible.

To boot, Billy Penn must have been enormously persuasive. In 1681, after only ten months of negotiation, King Charles II granted him 45,000 square miles on the Delaware River to settle a debt owed to his father's estate he had with his admiral father, William Penn Sr. The grant was named Pennsylvania ("Penn's Woods") in honor of Billy Penn's father, William Penn.

⊷⇒ ⇐⊷

When William Penn Sr.'s son, William Jr, (a/k/a Billy Penn) founded Penn's Woods (later called Pennsylvania), it was meant to be part of his "Holy Experiment." The aim of the young God-fearing Quaker was to establish a place where peace and toleration among peoples – including Indians – would bring harmony and prosperity; a moral society in which no one would be persecuted for his beliefs. The inhabitants would be free to make their own laws and to live like a "sober and industrious people."

Young Billy, believing that God would bless his colony as "the seed of a nation," sought as recruits for his colony those with a variety of occupational skills. Those who would share his ideals and take an active part in shaping his Experiment. To bring that to bear, Penn granted 500-acre parcels of woodland to certain of his recruits, from which the grantees would carve out a living. He favored most of all the God-fearing, hard-working Old Order Amish people from the Rhineland region of Germany.

The Old Order, who stuck tenaciously to the "old ways," were by comparison a radical sect. They saw in their old ways a strong sense of community responsibility, just what Billy Penn had been looking for!

⊷⇒ ⇐⊷

Penn's early recruits were free to make their own laws. He imposed few rules upon them, only those rules having to do with living in harmony with their fellowmen. Penn said further that there would be no distinction between the Quakers and the English (all those who were not Quakers).

The young Penn favored most of all "those God-fearing and hard-working" Amish people that came from Germany's Rhineland region. The Old Order, who stuck tenaciously to their "old ways," were by comparison a "radical sect" who closely guarded their "old ways." That took in a strong sense of community responsibility, just what Penn was looking for. In time he relegated "Friends" to recruit these people and to create a *new world* for them, another "world" free from the religious persecution they had been facing from the non-Amish in that region.

In dealing with the Indians already in Pennsylvania, Penn had two chief concerns: establishing trade and gaining title to land in a peaceful manner. *"Indians and English must live together in love as long as the sun gives light,"* he mandated. *"My grantees must not affront, nor in any way wrong, any Native American under penalty of law."*

In addition to the local Lenape, Penn also negotiated lands from the native Susquehannocks. There the young man envisioned a "Second Philadelphia" on the Susquehanna. He sold lots on the Susquehanna to English settlers, but he wasn't able to draw many English "Quakers" to the Susquehanna lands.

⊷══◐ ◑══⊷

From 1682 until 1754, Pennsylvania prospered. Young Penn's "Holy Experiment" under which diverse peoples would live together in peace, attracted peace-seeking Moravians and Mennonites from Europe. In even greater number, he attracted the Irish, the German Lutheran and the German Reformed (Calvinist) immigrants.

In Pennsylvania's so-called "attractiveness" also lay its "fatal flaw." While many of the Germans were welcomed by fellow

Germans already in the New World, the Scots-Irish, who by their nature were scrappy and inharmonious, had nowhere to go.

By the 1750's Pennsylvania had virtually closed its frontier. By then the native-born Pennsylvanians were competing with thousands of immigrants. Most of these immigrants had been driven out of Europe by poverty and religious persecution.

In turn, these same immigrants were lured by Pennsylvania propagandists, beginning with Billy Penn himself, who had assured them that land in colonial Pennsylvania was both "plentiful and cheap." At the same time the colonial "land of opportunity" was filling up fast. By the end of the 18th century, half of the people in eastern Pennsylvania had to work on someone else's land.

In the meantime there was also a *spiritual* side to settling for the original colony's founders. The spiritual element had been facing "decay" from the first. No society in the world could ever have fulfilled the founder's soaring hopes of Penn's "Holy Experiment."

Beginning with Penn's Quaker system of religious tolerance, a haven for those *low in the world,* Pennsylvania retained a unique religious profile. German and Swiss immigrants had been bringing their Old Order Amish Anabaptist traditions and settling in farm communities throughout Lancaster County and other areas of southeastern Pennsylvania.

As a group, these folk strongly believed in the redemptive power of humility, simplicity, basic non-competitiveness, and in withholding and protecting community traditions. Their belief worked so well with the *general spirit of the Holy Experiment* and in *keeping peace with the Indian,* that the same system has allowed this small sect to remain intact over several centuries.

Denominational variety marked the "religious" landscape in Pennsylvania. Churchgoing was a regular affair. Especially in rural Pennsylvania where churchgoing had evolved into a time for social gathering as well as a time for worshipping.

The Old Order Amish preferred to worship in their homes. Even after the establishment of meetinghouses, schools, and seminaries by the different religious groups, those of the Old Order still chose to worship in this way. To this day, they have been struggling to maintain their own system of personal beliefs and have been fighting to keep their own system of education.

Chapter 4

Exile

Once again the Master opened His hand to the youthful Samuel Fisher. Billy Penn offered him a grant of land in his woods *"across the Big Water"* known as Penn's Woods, later to be called *Pennsylvania*. Still in prison shackles, the Prison Superintendent ordered that Samuel be "exiled" at once. The prisoner was relieved of his shackles forthwith and placed aboard a cargo ship bound for the New World.

Freed from the prison and the Catacombs, Samuel now wore an entirely different hat. *"As I sail slowly toward my freedom, I know that if I do not leave my bitterness and hatred behind, I may as well still be in the Catacombs!"*

With too much time on his hands inside the lowly cabin of the ship, young Samuel had all the time in the world to concentrate on the helter skelter life he had been leading since leaving the Lowlands farm.

It seemed like only yesterday when Samuel took advantage of his father's failing health to bilk his brother out of the blessing of his forefathers. He had become deeply jealous when his mother did not have enough loving attention for both of her boys. "It still hurts!"

The twins were six when their mother died of birthing complications from which she never recovered. In a short time, the distraught widower married for the second time. Immediately life changed for everybody. The stepmother immediately adored Samuel, because he was the image of his father, both in stature and demeanor.

In turn, the new mother resented the fair haired, house bound Jacob and no longer wanted him underfoot. Jaob spent most of his waking hours walking alone throughout the fields, not aware of the anger and resentment toward his brother Samuel.

The boys were ten when their father became gravely ill. He called his new wife to his bedside. I am not much longer for this world. Bring Jacob to me and lay his lay him across my breast. I need to bless him.

"The youngster Jacob is not here," the stepmother lied. When he comes I will help you carry forth the sacred blessing."

"Climb onto your father's breast," the stepmother whispered to Samuel instead.

Samuel climbed down and stood at his father's bed. "You have blessed me, my father. I did what my stepmother said, and you have blessed me abundantly!"

"Samuel! But how can this be, my son!"

"You have deceived me!" Christian cried out to his wife. "My sons will be forever be accursed by the tainted blessing. You are sending me to an early grave!"

⊷═◯ ◯═⊷

All his life, Samuel Fisher remembered his father's angry words like he was hearing them only yesterday. And he remembered all too well his own exchange with his stepmother when he had reached the *age of accountability.*

"On this day you will take responsibility for the affairs of your family," the stepmother had told Samuel. "By your father's *Blessing,* you will inherit the land for this generation, then one day you will pass the blessing to your own youngest son."

But my dying father's *Blessing* rightfully belongs to my brother! It is not mine to own nor to pass forth," the young Samuel argued in spite of the pleas of a stepmother trying to defend her wrongdoing.

Samuel at all times refused to perform the responsibility because it was not his. The stoic Jacob stuffed his anger and vowed revenge. Samuel did his best to live above the bitter resentment Jacob carried toward him.

"I never wanted the blessing," Samuel argued with his stepmother. "I can not carry the banner for my generation. And I cannot pass the blessing down!"

"You *will* carry the banner for your generation, and you *will* pass the blessing down!"

⤙══◯ ◯══⤚

In time a bitter enmity was bred between the sons of Christian G. Fisher. Each went his own way, but the sibling struggle did not let up. Jacob stuffed his silent resentment down inside and behaved passive-aggressively toward his brother. Samuel, the outgoing one, put on a pretend happy face to hide the guilt for "stealing" the *Blessing*.

Samuel's carefree attitude got him through his youth, albeit without consortium with his brother. Jacob concerned himself with the affairs of the church by becoming self-righteous, while Samuel took on the life of the free-wheeler. However his freewheeling eventually to criminal behavior.

All throughout his youth Samuel suffered the rejection of a self-righteous brother and envied his standing in the church. No matter how hard Samuel tried, he could not earn grace in his brother's eyes, who carried a silent rage and vindictiveness and covered it with busyness in the affairs of the church. At the same time, Jacob envied Samuel's carefree spirit and longed for greater levity in his own life.

In the meantime, Samuel hid the pain of rejection by slowly and deliberately reverting to the *lowlife*.

⊷═◉ ◉═⊶

The estranged brothers hoped for things to get better between them, that each could forgive the other his transgressions and forget their differences. But their Amish stoicism kept either of them from making a start. Perhaps neither knew how.

Jacob wanted to accept his brother in spite of what had taken place with the blessing, but stayed stuck in the negative belief that what he had done was an abomination against God and the forefathers. Jacob was helpless to do anything except to stuff his anger and hide behind a false piety.

Samuel was caught in an emotional web of his own. He lived with two besetting sins – the lust for approval and the lust for control. He longed for the approval his estranged brother could not give him, and for the control he thought he was entitled to as the older brother. Neither lust could be satisfied, so he thought binges of drinking and public misconduct would help him compensate. Not one to contain emotion at such times, the young man let his emotions them out in all the wrong ways, at the expense of whoever happened to be around.

⊷═◉ ◉═⊶

Most mornings Samuel spent contemplating an uncertain future off in some strange world. He could not imagine what the second-class citizen found appealing. But Samuel easily repented such thoughts. *"My brother will love the changed man next time he sees me."*

Now that he had left the penitentiary, he missed his brother even more than he did when he was first incarcerated. He was on his way to begin life a world apart, and little did he know that the love-hate relationship the two would only continue to escalate.

The young voyager's mind became obsessed with being re-accepted in his brother's eyes. To become one with his estranged brother was paramount throughout the journey and gave him no rest. He would do it by becoming successful in the New World and winning back favor from his resentful brother. "Kill him with kindness," Guru Visser would have said. "Whatever that meant."

On board the cargo ship to the New World, Samuel found himself longing for his "good old days." He felt smothered in his tiny cabin and romanticized how good it must be to still be in the Old Country. *"All I can do is pray for prosperity off in the New World!"*

Far more significant was the degree to which Samuel longed for his brother Jacob's young son, with whom he had eagerly looked forward to reuniting after release from prison. The lad was named *Samuel,* for his uncle.

Samuel adored the young man named in his honor. From the lad's infancy, his admiring uncle played with him and tossed him above his head, giving him the love and attention a contentious mother and self-absorbed father did not know how to give. Everyone called him *Sammy II.*

Sammy II had been devastated when he learned that his Uncle had disappeared into some penitentiary, suddenly and with no explanation. The young lad worried ceaselessly over his uncle when the two were first separated.

After the ten-year-old Sammy II learned that his Uncle Sam was on his way to the ends of the earth, he wondered whether his uncle didn't love him any more and whether he would ever see his revered uncle again. Young Sammy II suffered his own kind of rejection.

"Everyone who has been a human child has felt a common terror," says a famous writer. "The greatest terror a child can have is that he is not loved, and rejection is the hell he fears. I think everyone in the world to a large or small extent has felt that kind of rejection. With rejection comes anger, and with anger some kind of crime in revenge for the rejection, and with the crime guilt; and that is the story of mankind."

They say that once a boy suffers rejection of that sort, he will find rejection even where it doesn't exist. Worse yet, he will draw even more rejection forth from people simply by "expecting" it! Sammy II felt a silent rage, such as any ten-year-old could feel, so suddenly and finally separated from his hero.

Part Two
The New World

Chapter 5

Billy Penn's New World

" **M** y land is a wilderness," Billy Penn instructed his newest subjects. "The virgin woods are crawling with both terror and excitement. There will be Indians to fight or deal with. We are seeking people that are tougher-skinned than all the rest. People who live close to the land and conduct their lives like pioneers. A severe test of any person's mettle!"

In spite of what young Penn had told his newest subjects, when Samuel Fisher came to the Pequea area he came upon a place of abundance. A place blessed with the song of birds and endowed with a balance of nature. The woods teemed with game for every table, especially the grouse and the colorful pheasant.

On every hand there was mature timber, ready and waiting to become someone's shelter from the winter cold. For centuries the timber had grown to maturity. Over the years the timber "harvested itself" with frequent lightning strikes, old age, and with decaying into the ground, making the soil rich and black. Everywhere, the woods was vibrant with the potential for future life.

Samuel Fisher's "place of abundance" bordered the Pequea Creek, a meandering creek originating with a series of perpetual springs in an area of Lancaster County called the Welsh Mountain, some fifty miles west of Philadelphia. The Creek meandered lazily east to west through the what was later named Lancaster County and emptied into the larger Susquehanna River at a small town called Pequea, named after the Indian tribe that settled there and gave the creek its name.

The Pequea was a gentle creek. All through the county, small "runs" flowed out of higher ground and fed into the creek. All along its banks the weeping willows reached out over the water, some so far they collapsed into the creek after an eroding bank could no longer contain the roots. Fish migrated upcreek from the Susquehanna, and the fishing was excellent. An abundance of fur-bearing muskrats and other water life burrowed into the hoary weeds all along the creek bed. So present and vibrant was the Pequea Creek that it touched the lives of all who lived in its vicinity.

⋇⟞⟝⟞ ⟝⟞⟞⋇

Young Samuel Fisher had been ambivalent about migrating to the New World, and it made his journey uncertain. Nonetheless, it was exciting enough, not knowing what was coming. At the same time it was frightening. He landed at Philadelphia, the bustling city of William Penn Sr and his family, including his son Billy. Just knowing a familiar face was going to at the dock to greet Samuel as he was arriving on the cargo vessel, would have taken a lot of the worry off the young voyager.

Alas, Billy was not at the dock to meet Samuel's vessel. Young Penn had gone to an area fifty miles west, to meet up with his other land grantees. Without a familiar face to greet him, Samuel felt displaced and wondered what he had gotten himself into. *"Maybe the Master doesn't want me here after all!"* he lamented, returning to the ship to spend another night in his cramped cabin.

Early the following morning the youthful pioneer began his long trek westward on what was US Highway 30 to the area where Billy Penn was setting aside grants of land for those he favored who were migrating from the Old Country to participate in his "Holy Experiment." The stage met up with Billy at a place called "Gap in the Hills," east of where Samuel's 500-acre grant of land was to be located.

◆⟐ ⟐◆

From the time Samuel Fisher set out for the New World, he faced adversity: billowing winds, unappetizing food, and disabling sickness aboard a cargo ship. A reluctant voyager to begin with, he spent hours alone in contemplation and self-examination. *"Surely I have displeased my Maker in leaving the Old Country!"*

Nonetheless, Samuel was eager for whatever was to come. It had been a painfully long voyage across the Big Water, cramped into small quarters aboard some cargo vessel. *"This life is a formidable task!"*

However, a driving force constrained the young pioneer to keep pushing forward. In time he would discover what it was that was driving him. *"Someday I will reconcile with my estranged flesh and blood, a mission I have been keeping alive by my own personal shame!"*

◆⟐ ⟐◆

The young missionary Billy Penn pointed toward a tract on the south side of the Conestoga Road, now US Highway 30, the Highway leading westward out from Philadelphia. The tract stretched clear from south of the "Big Highway" all the way down to the Pequea Creek. Needless to mention, young Samuel Fisher experienced a fresh new surge of energy!

The trees rose up out of rich, dark limestone soil and stood strong and straight. "You will push back the woods and prepare the land for tilling," Billy had instructed his grantees as they were leaving the Old Country.

"You will do well in your New World," Billy told Samuel before returning for his home in Philadelphia. "You possess clever hands and a creative mind." Thoroughly schooled in prison and aboard ship, then encouraged by Billy Penn's words to boot, Samuel wasted no time with feeling sorry over the meager tools and endless task of preparing for a long winter, now only a few months away.

—⇒ ⇐—

Young Samuel eagerly walked out to Highway US30 to meet with Penn's agent and a surveyor. With plot plan in hand, Penn's agent asked to walk around the boundary of his grant so that Samuel could find his bearing and establish the corners. *"I'd rather walk around by myself,"* he told the agent and surveyor.

Instead Samuel chose to wander by himself among the trees, get his own feel for the area, and continue to savor the freedom apart from the ship and the penitentiary before that. All day he closely examined his new property, running into something new every moment. He thanked his Creator for every tree and every grain of soil, grateful to be part of Penn's "Holy Experiment."

—⇒ ⇐—

On the north side of US Highway 30 lay a sleepy farm and railroad village. Samuel sought shelter in the village while he cleared enough ground for his own shelter. He began life with a crude lean-to, hoping to beat the severe winter that lay ahead.

It took Samuel no time to hook up with neighbors, eager to lend axe and crosscut saw in exchange for his new fellowship. Several of his newly-found neighbors worked together to perform a day's task, sharing muscle power, equipment and vision, utilizing some of the excellent people skills the youngster developed during penitentiary days.

The enterprising young pioneer lay awake long before the dawn broke, excited about all there was to reach for out there. He and his soft-spoken host barely exchanged words, while the vivacious hostess plied him with an early dish of grits and eggs.

After breakfast, the newest land grantee walked from the village toward the Pequea Creek in search of his bearing. He wandered along the creek to the place he thought were his land's boundary limits, then headed north to another boundary. So on until he had trodden every limit of his land grant. Now and then he leaned into a tall tree and peered up through the branches and foliage as though seeking the wisdom of his Master. By noon he had found a level spot in the protection of the trees which he fancied would one day become his "homestead."

To capture the feel for the bounds of his hoped-for homestead, Samuel took out his hunting knife and notched a tree here and there to mark the perimeter. He cut away the saplings and piled up the undergrowth. "Not very big, but enough so I'll find it in my next trip," he said of the clearing, before fashioning three fallen logs into a three-cornered fire pit and piling it high with the newly-cut saplings and undergrowth.

He sat nearby and imagined what his uncertain future might be. "But for the grace of God and the love of His people, where I drum up the courage to sit alone in a strange forest and dream of what the future might be?" he reasoned, grinding his boots into the gravel.

Back at the boarding house, Sam collapsed onto his cot. Hours of examining his land grant, communing with the Master, and just thinking as he walked back to the village, had done the youthful pioneer in. He had not eaten since early morning but was too exhausted to care. The sun was still up when he fell into the sleep of exhaustion.

The second morning, Samuel remained worn down from his first day. Excited with the prospects of a new one, Samuel headed back to his property while it was still dark. It was first-blackbird time; the grass was beginning to green around little pools of melting snow. *"Today I'll spend more time thinking and less time walking, before this out-of-shape body falls into disrepair.*

Armed with axe and crosscut saw borrowed from friends in the village, Samuel walked directly to the clearing. With renewed vigor, he chopped and sawed away enough space for a small clearing. All morning he wrestled with the tender young saplings, bending them together and binding the tops to form the image of a crude-looking dome. Beside himself with excitement and forgetting the tiredness from the day before, he took enough debris from the fire pit to fashion a roof. Several grunts and strains later, Samuel had blocked out the sunlight and had himself the makings of a shelter. By mid-afternoon he walked back to the boarding house, proud of the accomplishment of the second day.

With all that daylight to spare, he could not contain the excitement and hurried back to the clearing, armed with a skillet and battered cooking pan borrowed from the boarding house. "Not so much for the cooking as to make my shelter look like home!"

Once more Samuel slept the sleep of exhaustion.

→══◎　◎══←

On the morning of the third day, Samuel slowly ambled from the boarding house and headed for his new shelter with a rolled-up bearskin for the door of his "house," and dried rations for the "pantry." Grateful and armed with fresh resolve, the young pioneer Samuel headed for the clearing to continue clearing underbrush. He tingled inside his skin at the prospect of spending his first night in his new shelter.

Coming upon the clearing, he found that the shelter had been leveled, and the utensils gone!

For the first time since leaving the Catacombs, young Samuel Fisher was in unfamiliar surroundings and without a predictable routine. Gripped with fear, he gathered up his blanket and rations and scampered back to the village. *"I'll do my thinking there."*

Back at the boarding house, Samuel lay across his bunk with his hands behind his head like some country bumpkin and looked up through the ceiling for a new revelation. So often he had the same thing, first in the Catacombs, then in the cargo ship, and now at a boarding house. *"I gotta take my mind away from myself and get busy with useful things to do in the village!"*

⊹⇒◎ ◎⇐⊹

Several days after arriving in the New World, Samuel had been offered a place to live on a farm near his property. He faced the hard farm labor with a joy that rose above anything resembling the slightest burden. So engrossed was he with serving the farmer and his family that he put aside any responsibility he felt his own ground, except for an occasional stroll within the boundaries.

Samuel marveled at the beautiful dirt and trees in his place, but he did not go near the open space for sense of fear that was lurking there. So he remained content to till the soil, not so much for himself as for serving his new master. *"It's in giving that I receive,"* he remembered from his prison days, grinding his boots into the ground beneath his feet.

In an effort to combat fear and to attach to unfamiliar surroundings in the New World, Samuel resolved to strike a new acquaintance every other day. *"It worked pretty good while I was friendless back in the prison yard!"* Samuel Fisher as a natural servant in his own right Now combined with the people skills he brought from the penitentiary, this was the best resolution young Samuel could come up with.

Getting out and extending himself was resolution enough after all the mornings when he went directly from bed to work on his land grant. Every day he arose from his bed with renewed vigor. With his friendly spirit and renewed purpose, he drew people to himself like flies to honey. The resolution took him above and beyond what he could have asked for or imagined, like mounting on wings of an eagle and soaring on the heights.

Now Samuel had an unknown, bewildering fear to contend with in his new world. Nevertheless, he had been brave and an overcomer. Or so he thought.

⋯⇥⊙ ◯⇤⋯

Word had spread rapidly about the young Amish man who had arrived as part of Billy Penn's "Holy Experiment." When local folk learned that he had been granted land between the village and the Pequea Creek, the "bewhiskered young Quaker" gained instantaneous favor with the local people, who extended to him a spirit of cooperation.

After shying away from his own place in the woods for a time, Samuel decided to brave it and walk directly into the clearing for another "visit." He had grown to love tilling the land for the neighboring farmer. Now he had returned to his own place with renewed spirit. *"But it feels too much alone,"* declared Samuel after he left his place of employment.

"Sure could use 'abody to plan with and talk to," he said as he notched boundary trees with his hunting knife. *"Someone I could trust to walk with through this formidable task."*

From the time Samuel first walked into his woods, he did not "feel" the young Indian spying on him from a nearby tree.

⊷⇒ ⇐⊷

Some months after working as a hired hand and his boss's rather casual mention of the land grant, Samuel's benevolent employer summoned together the muscle power of hard-working consortion, often merry-making of friend and neighbor. "A frolic to clear the land," the boss suggested, borrowing a concept from The Old Country

Beginning at Bachman's Lane the neighbors and friends cleared a swath a lane's width in the direction of a clearing Samuel had earlier told the farmer he had planned for an eventual homestead. Logs were piled along the swath. Lots of local camaraderie came with the labor of the frolic, and the young pioneer was deeply humbled by the labor his new friends and neighbors were putting into the land-clearing frolic.

Samuel had resolved not to go to the clearing, not even on the day of the frolic, after the raids to his shelter. But he finally relented. "I'm going to the clearing no matter what," he asserted, expecting to find his place a shambles and imagining a savage confrontation. He was mystified by what he found.

The arrow was still stuck through the door. Samuel was disappointed in himself for not staying with his project, in spite of the earlier attacker. *"Who was this most recent raider? More friendly than hostile, I hope!"*

On the day of the frolic, young Samuel struck up acquaintance with friends he would not otherwise have, had it not been for the frolic. His faith increased and carried him on eagle's wings. *"Coincidence? Providence?"* Meanwhile he kept up his diligent efforts as a live-in hired hand.

At the frolic Samuel had worked alongside the local implement dealer. "Come see me anytime you need to borrow something for your project here," the dealer offered.

"I haven't done much of anything on the project," Samuel told the dealer. "I ran into a snag." The dealer was too busy to care about any snag and the matter was dropped.

But Samuel's mind stayed with the implement dealer. "I need somebody to talk to about problems down at my property," Samuel told the dealer from time to time.

"I'm listenin'." Samuel explained as best he could.

"An arrow? Hmm. Somebody don't want you around there. Some unfriendly Indian, I reckon. Now and then a Pequea Indian squats on a piece of ground and decides that he owns it. Prob'ly what's happenin' on your piece. I'll put my ear to the ground for you."

"Sure 'nuf," said the dealer when he spied Samuel in the field. "Appears a lone Susquehannock family paddled off the Susquehanna at the town of Pequea and laid claim to land that happens to be some of yours. Reckon you got yourself an unfriendly neighbor you have to stand up to."

"I will not fight and jeopardize my relationship with the peace-loving Quakers."

"Then I reckon ya gotta kill your new enemy with kindness."

--=○ ○=--

The implement dealer must have increased the young man's faith because that weekend he decided to be daring and to hang out at his project. He even dared remove the arrow to examine the sharpened flint and turkey feathers and go back inside the shelter.

The blanketed bed of leafy underbrush was undisturbed. He lay on the nest and thanked his Creator for protecting him from the unknown, hoping his prayers would find their way up through the intersecting poles.

Samuel "slept awake" and with ears open, until renewed hunger pangs prodded him out of a fitful sleep. He had not perceived of any night intruder. "No one to kill with kindness." He stuck the arrow back in the door and returned to the farm to resume his duties as the hired hand. By day's end, he had somehow summoned the courage to go sleep in his leanto one final time before deciding what he was going to do next.

In the meantime Samuel's visitor had struck again. This time the arrow was not sticking through the door. A momentary fear paralyzed him. But he parted the bearskin and stooped through the doorway before collapsing onto the blanket of leaves, exhausted from yet another day of farm labor.

"Something's different here!" The cooking pot and utensils hung on vines from the ceiling in the semi-darkness. A second sense told Samuel that if there was indeed a threat, the attacker would have struck by this time. *"Matter of fact, my 'guest' has gotten less intrusive every time he comes."*

⤜⟹ ⟸⤛

The land clearing in from Bachman's Lane was indeed proving to be a formidable task, and word spread rapidly of a second frolic. The same faces appeared as in the frolic before, except for one who remained off to himself and labored extra hard. Now and then Samuel sensed the muscular, red-faced stranger observing him closely. A turkey tail-feather was pierced through a long black ponytail. Although Samuel and the stranger did not meet, he looked forward to adding him, his first Indian, to his growing list of recent new acquaintances.

It was the weekend following the frolic. Now that a swath had been cleared in from Bachman's Lane, Samuel went back to expanding the opening around his shelter. The young entrepreneur was so excited about his new venture that his enthusiasm trumped any earlier apprehension. *"One more night before I trust setting up my camp for good!"*

Before retiring to his lean to, Samuel's eye came upon something peculiar at the edge of the clearing. Somebody had carved into the trunk of a tree! The the light-colored carving on the darkened bark had caught the young pioneer's eye in the semi-darkness. *"Obviously an Indian symbol! Somebody is sending me a clear message."*

Samuel lay silently in his shelter, wishing he had become better acquainted with the red-faced Indian at the frolic. *"The Indian would interpret the message for me! Then anybody in the village can do it for me. I'm sure there will be more messages."*

"I am not in the New World to create enemies, but without a doubt I have been disturbing somebody's peace and quiet. But whose? Am I going to be my very first neighbor's enemy? Is he friendly or is he hostile?"

Samuel had only one way to find out the answer to his questions – by going about his business and not let fear hinder his progress. "I must jump right back in, right now, before I lose courage altogether, like a kid scared of remounting his horse after being thrown off."

Early the following morning, armed with new resolve and the same borrowed axe and saw, Samuel returned to the clearing and did indeed "jump right back in." He labored feverishly to enlarge the space planned for the eventual barn and house. Now and then he threw a furtive glance into the trees, trying best to ignore any thought of being spied upon. "The longer it goes 'til somebody ransacks me again, the less likely it's gonna happen," the wannabe pioneer rationalized to muster courage to keep going.

By the end of the week, fear of the unknown had all but passed. Samuel felt energetic, determined to keep pushing out the perimeter of his hoped-for homestead. He spent the Sabbath in meditation and in communion with his Creator, eager to continue his venture with renewed enthusiasm. At night he slept fitfully at best, elated with each prior accomplishment. "Maybe he decided to go away. I'll brave it out!"

Samuel faced his new week with increased boldness. Once again he pulled together the tops of several saplings and bound them with vines. From underbrush piled here and there, he thatched yet another covering. He left the inside untouched except to escape the hot afternoon sun. "No need for utensils, they're just gonna walk anyhow."

Samuel's work as hired hand was over for yet other the day. He headed for his estate, once more loaded with necessaries for making the shelter more liveable. This time he appeared armed with another blanket for his bed and yet another cowhide to close off the leanto. "My place will look better with a door," he said, covering up his fear.

As Samuel approached his place, he felt apprehensive from the time he had left there before. He was relieved to see his leanto intact as he walked into the cleared area. Peering into the leanto, Samuel was gripped with new fear. Someone had been in his house and piled together underbrush and leaves to form a bed. Someone spent the night in the leanto!

Samuel paid his squatter little mind as he hung the cowhide across the doorway. He kicked aside the bed of leaves, and set to making his own bed, determined not to be afraid to sleep in his own shelter the following night. With that done, he chopped away more brush to extend the margin of the clearing. Late afternoon he closed off the entrance and fell onto his blanketed leaf bed to see how it felt. He headed home with only axe in hand.

Samuel had entered the New World with a child-like pioneering spirit. He was confident he could fend for himself in the wilderness. But he was naive against the wiles of man, ill-equipped to handle a surprise like the one he found the next morning. Someone had stuck an arrow through the cowhide door!

First off, some culprit had taken the his cooking utensils and leveled the lean to. Now some invasive soul had spent the night on his leaf bed, to boot. And then came a message clear enough for anybody to understand. Obviously someone did not want the bearded young Quaker traipsing in his woods. The flint arrow, freshly honed, was a clear enough message from some hostile neighbor. Samuel, gripped with yet another fear, turned around and walked right back to the village to re-group and decide on a new course of action.

On another day Samuel ambled slowly from the clearing and down toward the Pequea. Near the creek he was caught spellbound by one large and majestic tree off to the side. He stood beneath the tree and beheld its gigantic arms spreading in all directions. So taken up was the young pioneer with the tree that he immediately broke a narrow path directly to the tree. *"My meditation tree. Where I shall go to visit with my Creator!"*

⊷⇒ ⇐⊷

A silent intruder watched closely as Samuel surveyed the trees right below him, curious that the young white man would have cut a narrow path to this particular tree. *"My tree, planted by the water, which yields its fruit in due season,"* the young white man mused. He would remember prophetically from *The Book of Psalms* every time he paid the majestic tree another visit.

The young man's excitement lasted into the night so that he caught himself "sleeping awake."

Around mid-morning Samuel took the narrow path he had cut the evening before and sat under the meditation tree. At the tree he discovered a newly-carved message in the side of the trunk – the same symbol as someone had carved into the tree at the edge of the clearing.

Samuel studied the carving. *"What's it say? Show thyself!"* He took out his pocket knife and carved a *cross* directly beneath the symbol he had just been studying. He returned back to work at the farm, excited about his own "mysterious message" and his answer to it.

The following morning the young pioneer returned to further expand the open space for his planned homestead. He took the narrow path to his meditation tree and studied the message that was left earlier in the day. *"Nary a soul responded to the message of the Cross,"* he pondered, giving poetic justice to the message.

He ran his fingers across the earlier carving and examined the edges. What he discovered piqued his curiosity anew. The message was inscribed by a sharply-honed arrowhead. *"Same as the one he had found stuck in his door?"*

Chapter 6

Big Heart (aka Grosse Hertz)

As Samuel was thus examining the message that had just been left for him, he was surprised by a deep voice from behind. "My personal message to you!" Samuel whirled around and looked squarely into the face of the exotic man that he had seen observing himself during the second frolic. Obviously a "local" Susquehannock.

Samuel stood frozen in place. *"What's it mean?"* His eyes remained fixed on the regal Susquehannock.

"It means I stand guard over your land."

All the time, the Indian had been carefully spying upon the goings-on of a young white man from a fork high in the "meditation tree" where he kept his lookout, high enough that no suspecting eyes would have detected him. Every day the Indian sat in the fork of the tree. Like a sentinel, he carefully guarded any activity up and down the Pequea, especially that of the newly-arrived white man with the red whiskers busily working on his project.

The Indian watched closely the young man's reaction each time he was made to deal the Indian's bizarre activity. The wisened Indian was aiming to test the young white man's mettle to the max, but the white man was "passing" every test!

Initially the young white man and the wisened old Susquehannock groped for words of common language. After "attacking" and exchanging their numerous words and phrases, the two began to strike what felt like an immediate "closeness." Not with a lot words, but with a certain depth of spirit. Before long, the white man began prospering under his grand old mentor!

"I worried over having to fight you, to drive you out," the old Indian said later. "Your people – the white ones – are driving my people out and putting us into reservations. But no man will drive me and my family out of these woods without a fight. Every day I had been watching you closely, and I like you. You are my kind of people." Samuel was too moved to say anything.

"My name for you shall forever be 'Grosse Hertz', meaning Big Heart!"

⊷═◉ ◎═⊶

Samuel lay stretched out on his leaf-cot, too excited to sleep, now that the phantom intruder was turning out to be more than friendly. In time the young pioneer found that he loved the old Susquehannock with an uncritical love, in the manner of dogs and children. And the feeling was mutual. It was as though the two could look into a creature's soul and soothe every wound they found there. *"I am sure I can trust this old Indian with even my deepest secrets!"*

"When cold comes, you're gonna need a better teepee," declared Big Heart as they rested from a day of chopping and clearing. "The white man is too frail for the elements we are used to. Let us build a better shelter -- 'hogan' to the white man."

The idea for the hogan comes from my Navajo brothers in the Great Southwest whose clever hands first invented the hogan out of earth and trees. The many sided structure of earth and timber is still the traditional dwelling of my Navajo people in the Great Southwest. We shall invent our own version of the many-sided structure where you will sleep in peace with Mother Earth and Father Sky.

All day Samuel and the old Susquehannock worked side by side to build the young white man's hogan. Big Heart began with fashioning a circle of logs around a fire pit. They hewed slabs from the trunks of saplings too young for logging and drove them into the ground around the pit.

They lashed the bottoms of the saplings together and secured them with vines, pulling the tops together and binding them roughly in the shape of a traditional teepee. With mud and grass, symbols of Mother Earth and Father Sky, they closed up the sides of the structure. Smoke and embers from the fire pit were pulled up through the center of the structure. "The sides of mud and grass will be replaced before the cold of winter comes to visit."

"Like living in a big round chimney, Grosse Hertz!"

Samuel and his Mentor sat silently around the fire. The Indian's headband and feather glowed in earth tones under his brown skin. "These are our Native American Ten Commandments." Big Heart spoke slowly but with great authority.

The Earth is our Mother; care for her.
Honor all your relations.
Open your heart and soul to the Great Spirit.
All life is sacred; treat all beings with respect.
Take from the Earth what is needed and nothing more.
Do what needs to be done for the good of all.
Give constant thanks to the Great Spirit for each new day.
Speak the truth; but only of the good of others.
Follow the rhythms of nature; rise and retire with the sun.
Enjoy life's journey, but leave no tracks.

The young white man's face remained downward in awe and reverence. Everything was changed for the better after Big Heart, "the rescuer" appeared. Where there had been fear for the young white man, now Big Heart was providing his own honest form of fellowship. Where there had once a form of darkness, there was vision. The regal Susquehannock was providing direction and stamping out confusion. Above all, the regal Indian was providing a long-lost hope in a strange land!

⭢▬▭ ▭▬⭠

Samuel and Big Heart walked down toward the creek. A few feet off the path stood a massive, stately tree with giant limbs and a huge, exposed root system that bound the trunk to the earth. The sprawling arms had a powerful, meditative presence, like a natural spirit. "Since the day I myself followed my way up this winding creek, this tree has always been my lookout. Members of my tribe believe this tree talks!"

Inside the newly-constructed hogan Big Heart had fashioned a seating area around the fire pit with an array of fallen logs. He gestured with his powerful chin. "Powwow place!"

"How's about finding me a companion, Grosse Hertz?"

"We will find a good one for you, Young Samuel! And if you cannot find a good companion to walk with, then walk alone. Like an elephant roaming the jungle. It is better to be alone than to be with those who hinder your progress. And now, maybe smoke a little pipe?"

Young Samuel tingled inside his skin at the thought of his first powwow with the regal Susquehannock!

⭢▬▭ ▭▬⭠

Samuel moved into the hogan and life immediately felt civilized. Out the back of his new *house,* which at had been formerly his *lean to*, he made a shed for tools accumulated from his many treks to and from the village.

At the opening to his hogan, Samuel proudly devised a table and chair and placed them at the opening where he could catch the light of day, in the bright morning light. Samuel stepped away to admire the work of his hands.

"No excuse not to write to my brother now!"

⊷⟹ ⟸⊷

One morning Big Heart appeared with a rake and hoe in hand. You have rich ground everywhere in your compound. The richness of your ground comes from the constant, slow recycling your virgin woods, caused by ages of of lightning strikes and of rotting wood finding its way into the ground and mixes with more rich materials.

Come the next growing time, the next renewal of life, I shall plant a small garden in your rich soil, by your grace. "This will be my first garden, Big Heart, my very first garden in my life anytime and anywhere!"

Our seasons are come from Mother Earth and Father Sky. Their union create our seasons things depending upon where we live. My brothers and sisters in the Southwest name their seasons according to significant time periods in their year. They name them loosely "Renewal of Life," "Wet Season," "Distant Travel," and "Wisdom."

In our parts, however, the different parts of the year, like "Spring Planting," "Sunshine," " Showers," " Fall Harvest," celebrate the cycles of life in our seasons.

My favorite things to grow in my garden, and now in yours, are squash, some kind of maize or corn, and climbing beans. When planted close together, these crops benefit each other and we refer to them as "Three Sisters Garden, a Native American practice.

Squash is the easiest crop to grow and cultivate. When planted together with its two sisters they help one another grow and care for each other. Both kinds of beans, the kind with vines that wants a lot of room to spread, and the kind that simply grows in a bush.

Feel free, Grosse Hertz. My land is your land!

Then I shall grow some kind of corn-like maize, at least two kinds of squash, and beans. I like work with both kinds of squash. The winter squash has a hard shell, like the rind of a pumpkin, and grows from a vine. You will enjoy eating it after I prepare it, especially when we roast it over an open fire. The summer squash has a soft rind and grows from a stalk, like the zucchini and the crookneck, the kind my people like to eat raw.

Squash is an Indian word you know. In the Native American, it means "to eat raw or uncooked." The hard kind, related to your pumpkin, comes from my Indian brothers in South America. At to my bean seeds, the Seneca seed, come from my Seneca brothers up north.

I shall also try my luck with the ancient Anasazi bean seeds. Thousands of years ago, the *Anasazi Indians* (called *Cliff-Dwellers*) grew a famous maroon and white bean as one of their main sources of food. With any luck at all with growing this warm-weather bean, we will cook with this very same bean used by the ancient Cliff-Dwellers and enjoy my famous "Cliff-Dweller bean soup!"

Samuel listened in amazement to all he was learning from his old mentor Susquehannock in the short while since he had first met him. Every day the young pioneer became more grateful for the day they became friends!

Big Heart's "Three Sisters Garden" grew by itself, and it grew like crazy. You could practically "hear" the vines growing overnight, so fast did the beans and the winter squash grow!

Big Heart had been absent for a number of days, observing the period for " Distant Travel." One day he visited the hogan with a surprise. "A wild turkey killed with my bow and arrow!"

To celebrate the trophy, Samuel built a fire pit near the front door of the hogan. Big Heart buried the turkey in the embers. All day the beautiful bird spat its fat into the embers. The smell of roasting turkey permeated both the inside and outside of the hogan.

At twilight Big Heart brought his family to meet Samuel. They ate with the grateful white man in his newly-built hogan and celebrated into the night. For days they feasted on turkey, cherishing every last leftover morsel.

When Samuel Fisher's predecessors arrived in the New World, they faced adversity from the start. Billowing winds, unappetizing food, and disabling sickness met them head-on, even as they headed out to sea. From the outset, the prospective colonists murmured, wondering if perhaps they had displeased their God by leaving their place in the Old Country.

The predecessors, a cross between Pirates and Puritans, not far removed from each other in that both had a strong dislike for opposition. Both clung to what they had and coveted what was not theirs. They obviously began with their hearts in the right place, desiring peace and pursuing it. They desired the pure in heart. Many did indeed possess purity of heart and showed it on the outside.

Others feigned purity on the outside but were far from pure on the inside. The impurity stayed hidden behind a veil of simple dress and sober demeanor.

Life abounded for the enterprising Samuel, He continued his pleasant demeanor in the village, making friends wherever he went.

He was never at a loss for volunteers to help with his project. When he found time away from his work as a hired hand, he worked at his own project, sometimes for only a few hours at the end of his day.

When he did find time to work on his own, some neighbor would come by to pitch in his muscle and might. As the clearing expanded into a few tillable acres, Samuel already visualized fields teeming with the fruits of his labor.

⊷�⊶

To prepare for the fast-approaching winter, Big Heart and Samuel replaced the mud and grass sides of the hogan with every wooden remnant they could come across. Every findable remnant to shear up the sides of the hogan against the impending winter cold.

Samuel replaced his nest of leaves and grass with a cot he had fastened to one side of the eight-sided structure. He covered the cot with a bearskin and topped it with a blanket he had borrowed from his farmer's wife. *"All set! Comfortable as the night is long; grateful as the given day!"*

Big Heart must been have on a roll. As one last added feature, also done in Samuel's absence, he quite artfully inscribed on the wooden wall above Samuel's head the following:

BLESSING

May the Warm Winds of Heaven
Blow softly upon your Hogan.
May the Great Spirit bless all who enter here.
May your Moccasins make Happy Tracks in many Snows
And the Rainbow always touch your Shoulder.

Samuel loved the hogan that he and Grosse Hertz had built. It provided a wonderful shelter – walls for the wind, a roof to sip tea beside a fire, and laughter to cheer you and all you love. Samuel was able to sleep every night without fear, after finishing his daily labors as a hired hand at a neighboring farm. Every night he thanked *The Great Spirit* for one more day of good health and of every kind of blessing. Life for Samuel was indeed looking up!

"I have indeed come upon my happy place, my place of Gemutlichkeit!"

⟶⟹ ⟸⟵

By the time Samuel Fisher came to the New World, his people had already begun settling in the area. A lazy creek meandered throughout the area and dumped into the Susquehanna River. The creek was named the *Pequea* by the Indian tribe already living in the "Village of Pequea." The region came to be referred to as the *Pequea Region*, the center for the *Pequea People*.

Early life was a time of rugged innocence and dogged persistence. It was hard enough work, carving out an honest living from a woodland in a hostile environment during the hardest of times. But everybody hung together to brave the elements – stifling summer heat, hard winters, all manner of disease, with an enemy lying in wait to steal, kill, and destroy.

The people brought with them to the New World a pioneer attitude born of persecution. They wrestled their strange new world like Jacob, grandson Abraham, had wrestled with his own angel. Looking to build their own Bethel, relentless and refusing to let go until God blessed them. "God has ordained the *Holy Experiment* and the battle is His," the people said and believed. So they fought their battles for God. And one day it would become their own "Land of Milk and Honey" later to be looked upon and referred to as "The Garden Spot of America."

Each had come from the *Das Alte Landt,* a/k/a the Old Country, persecuted for their beliefs. Although suppressed, each believed he was a natural-born survivor. These were real pioneers, rugged, stoic, aware of who they were. "Mainly chiefs and few Indians."

They started out like a nation of giants, invincible in their newly-found freedom from suppression, confident they could survive anything after the treacherous sea voyage from the Old Country. They came to attack the elements and carve a new land from a wilderness under Billy Penn's "Holy Experiment" attacking their mission without the benefit of anything convenient or modernized.

These were the most rugged of individualists, prepared to conquer the elements and clash headon with anything that might block their industry. From their beginnings in Germany, this quiet and gentle people lived close to the soil, grateful for the miracle of life and death, and for every seed that died into the ground and then rose to life.

Samuel Fisher was such a person. Long he hid the evil in his heart behind a plain garb and a sober and industrious spirit. But for him, evil militated against good so long and so hard that he lived in constant confusion of spirit. In his confusion he was barely able to separate church life from town life. In time he could barely distinguish his church people from his town friends, who loved him but misled him.

Young Samuel worked hardest of them all, harder than normal. He was driven by an inner vow he had carried from the Catacombs: "to be the head and not the tail."

Paramount was the young man's wish to reconcile with his brother Jacob.

⊷═◉ ◉═⊷

The Amish concept of religion was other-worldly and fiercely private, with fear of a mystical Higher Power, whose pleasure was obedience to the law of Moses. They possessed an abiding sense of *bruderschaft* (brotherhood) -- of sharing, agape love, "loving God with all your heart and your neighbor as yourself."

And of policing one another?

Denominational variety marked the religious landscape in Pennsylvania. Churchgoing was a regular affair. Especially in rural Pennsylvania where they made worship a time of social gathering as well as for worship itself.

According to custom, the Amish were a spiritual people – filled with beliefs they had carried with them from *Das Alte Landt*. Out from a "peasant mysticism" there arose their belief in a jealous, watchful God who meted out equal portions of reward and punishment in running His universe.

Upon this simple mysticism, the Old Order Amish formed their *Ordnung,* a vehicle for keeping "spiritual order" in the body of the church, that evolved into more of a "cultural order-keeping" and a way to preserve their culture.

The *Ordnung* was invented to keep the church body pure and was dictated by the church Elders. Each church district had its own "*Ordnung*" in general. Since all districts were fundamentally alike, the Ordnung created a consistency throughout Amish daily life that carried into the culture and evolved into an viable community.

The overall *Ordnung* was decided by, and made up for, those who practiced it. It was seldom questioned, although the degree of enforcement was. When dictated, it came across as stringent to one who chose to live more informally, encouraging such a one to weasel in and out of the watchful and judging eye of layman, elder or deacon.

All women wore floppy wide-brimmed hats then (forerunner of today's bonnet). The more haughty ones wore flowers on tops of their bonnets, with slits in the brims to bring a scarf up through and tie under the chin in severe weather.

Their women possessed a self-righteousness brought from *Das Alte Landt* that "allowed" them the right to gossip or backbite. "Being talked about" posed a real threat to the one thing they valued most – their respectability.

Each tried guarding her respectability with her very life. "To be gossiped about" about meant an erosion of a woman's respectability. If the woman was not respected, she was nothing. However if her man was not respected, it did not mean as much. He was the hunter. When the hunter was gone, his woman was expected to cover for him, careful not to let another woman talk her man down.

It stands to reason that the woman took the brunt of whatever was going down with her man. If he did learn that he was the subject of wags, he was able to shrug it off on his missus, getting peer support with it. The husband was superior to his missus for being the hunter and explorer, and for that he got her protection and respectability.

The men-- hunters and protectors-- went about their business and didn't care a lick what the women said and did. If a man was the unfortunate subject of gossip, it was done quietly because it was about one of their own. However, when the gossip was of someone "outside" the circle, the women went at it whole hog. The men could leave the gossip alone, realizing that when a story simmered down, the wags would find another circumstance to pounce upon or a new person to devour.

Opinions flew through the Colony like a house afire. One neighbor talked to the other, each repeating half and adding fuel to a never-ending cycle. The women were always right, they thought, even when they were dead wrong, and one day gossip evolved into a cultural thing. Cultural in that it became an "accepted" way of life; cultural in that it seemed right even though it was harmful. Cultural in that it became the pulse of the community--a two-edged sword, piercing asunder the very fabric that was meant to keep them in line!

As life took on meaning in Penn's Woods, Samuel's thoughts turned more and more to his brother Jacob back in the Old Country. His heart ached to be right with his estranged brother. Even at the end of his best day, the unfinished business with Jacob gnawed at him. The blues visited him by day and the pain remained stuffed deep within a hurting spirit. He tried to compensate for the blues and pain with extreme labor, but they merely got worse because there was no way to bring it out and talk about it.

Samuel wished in the worst way to confide in Big Heart to lessen some of his pain and guilt, but he could not find words to broach the subject.

One day as Samuel and Big Heart powwowed around the fire pit, Sam decided, once and for all, to bring up the subject of his brother, hoping that the two could share a few heart-to-heart matters. Samuel began by talking vaguely of a brother in the Old Country and of an estranged relationship, barely letting Big Heart in. Their so-called "sharing" failed miserably when Samuel became reluctant to divulge *anything* to Big Heart. The Indian listened patiently to his young white friend but did not push him.

So the young white man continued to suffer in lonely silence. But the wizened old Susquehannock could *hear* his pain!

⇥⇤

Regret over things long past hounded Samuel relentlessly, keeping him awake at night and daydreaming by day. *"I want for my brother and his family to come to the New World,"* he finally told Big Heart. *"I need him here!"*

"You must let go of the past, or you're gonna miss tomorrow!"

"*Regardless of the past, I want my brother and his family here. Right now! I will my best to get them to join me here in the New World!*"

At the same time, Samuel had no way of knowing what to expect from the brother and his family; or from himself, for that matter. "*How would I prepare if they did agree to come?*"

"Where's your faith?"

"*My faith is pretty fragile.*"

"I've heard it said, let your faith increase and you will soar on wings, like an eagle!"

"*Rejection is the thing I suffer most from my brother in the Old Country.*"

"Doesn't surprise me. Rejection often comes from those who matter most to us; and who matters more to you than the one you've been with from the time your mother carried you in her belly."

"*Enough said already, Grosse Hertz!*"

On his next trip to the village, Samuel came back with pen and ink. He sat at the table and looked through the opening of his new place, bombarded with question after question. "*What shall I say after all this time? Does he know I am released from prison and living somewhere over the water in some strange New World? If my letter does reach him, would he acknowledge that I even tried to made contact? How often do I write him before I can invite him to join me in the New World?*"

The faithful Susquehannock continued to work alongside Samuel on occasion. When he sensed that Samuel was over-extending, they would retire to the hogan to powwow and smoke. Samuel relied upon such times for his well-being. He kept a pile of embers smoldering just for the powwows.

"*How could I ever make it without the faithful Grosse Hertz? Yet I can not find the words to open up about to him about my long-lost brother!*"

"We smoke to your long-lost brother," suggested Big Heart, as though reading Samuel's mind.

"What's there to smoke about!"

Big Heart sensed the pain. "In true Native American fashion, he did not bring up the subject again. Young Samuel respected the old Susquehannock with a uncritical love, a love that he had never before felt for another person.

⊷⩫ ⩭⊷

Samuel continued to stuff his feelings about Jacob deeper and deeper inside. The more he stuffed his feelings, the harder he worked to compensate for the gnawing pain. Now and then he could actually "notice" that his spirit was changing. Sometimes the mix of changes bewildered him.

He sensed himself becoming successful. The more he sensed the success, the more successful he dreamed of becoming. As success begat success, his life seemed to spiral out of control and his faith began to wane. He feared both success and failure and was frightened of his own shadow.

"I simply must *go talk to someone, somebody I can open up to!"* His spirit no longer allowed him to open up to Big Heart after he had rebuffed him at the last powwow.

Alone with his thoughts, Samuel's depression got far worse to where it was difficult to concentrate at the project he once loved so dearly. There were mornings when he awoke from a fitful sleep without energy to face the new day. He tried for all he was worth to flee from his demons, but he thought he could never outdistance them. He started to keep his friends at arm's length for fear of appearing vulnerable.

Unfortunately for Samuel, he had brought a stable of demons with him from the Old Country. He thought he had to fight the demons alone in an already hostile environment. *"Day after day I remove stumps to carve farmland out of a wild forest, while back in the*

Old Country my brother goes along softly and gently, sowing and watering with joy." Obviously he felt sorry for himself for having to carry such a lion's share of work at the same time he was grappling his personal demons.

The negative thoughts would come only in down moments, and that disturbed young Samuel even more. The thoughts and expressions stirred up hatred and invited strife. Yet in his good moments, he was confident he loved his brother as he did himself.

Shuffling along the path to his hogan, it occurred to him what Big Heart had suggested earlier on, how that in giving we receive. *"But what shall I give my brother?"*

The plan hit like a thunderbolt. *"I will give to Jacob by bringing him to the New World, to a place of new beginning. I will give him the gift of forgiveness! Never mind whether he gives it to me or not, I will give it to him anyhow. I will even build him a homestead. Right here within the Colony!"*

All that night, Samuel lay at the opening of his hogan and listened to the singing of the crickets!

◦⇒ ⇐◦

When Samuel Fisher became friends with the Susquehannock Big Heart, he took a major stride toward the prosperity he now learned to enjoy. Big Heart and his warrior son spent a lot of time with Samuel after he provided shelter for the Indian and his family, helping him harvest trees for lumber and clearing land for tilling.

The Susquehannock blessed Samuel all the more by bringing his friends to meet him, lending muscle power and humor. He had very few low times during the days he spent with *Grosse Hertz* and his warrior son.

Most of Samuel's successes rode the crest of intense mood swings. During an upper, he was able to "garner" the inertia of several people. During such an upper, there was no stopping the man whose real energy was about compensating for past wrong and feelings of inadequacy. The stigma aroused by gossips over "the time the young man spent in prison" didn't help matters.

Few people knew out about Samuel's more violent mood swings. Even fewer could have perceived the reason for them. But since the sensitive young man revealed what he had done by sneaking onto the breast of his dying father, he was tormented by a deep inner need to assuage the remorse he carried with him, like some grievous backpack.

Samuel became obsessed with the need to prove himself worthy of the *blessing* that actually belonged to Jacob which he and his stepmother had appropriated by deceit many years ago.

When his spirit was "up and running", he was a natural leader. His tall stature and piercing eyes enhanced his people skills and bode him well. At the same time, there were those who neither acknowledged his "people power" nor respected any opinion coming from him. "Got no time for the kid's half-baked ideas," said Joe Feree, self-proclaimed community leader.

Young Samuel had to struggle for a place in Joe Feree's eyes. At the same time, he was among those who tipped their steins on a Saturday afternoon. During his surge in prosperity, Samuel became a highly esteemed member in the Pequea church district and throughout the settlement as well.

$\Longleftrightarrow$

During spring thaw, Samuel summoned the collective muscle power of his church to throw together the frame of his first barn. The Amish called it "our *frolic* for young Sam Fisher." Later in the spring, he called together his English friends and neighbors to further boost his efforts in construction. The English called it *"our barn-raising for young Sam Fisher."*

Samuel developed a knack for summoning a spur of the moment get-together. He had numerous other of like get-togethers during the spring season. People of all kinds enjoyed working together to combine muscle power for the enterprising young Fisher--from felling timber and turning it to lumber, to clearing brush to increase the tillable acreage.

With lumber and plans and people always in place, a get-together turned like efficient clockwork under the quiet yet forceful leadership of the likeable man they referred to as the young Pequea Sam Fisher.

⊷═◯ ◯═⊷

Pequea Sam's new prosperity spread its influence outside the settlement as well. The meandering Pequea Creek became known for its many crossings thoughout the agricultural country-side. The enterprising Sam Fisher jockeyed into position with the lumber brokers, providing them with heavy planking to construct covered bridges at points along the meandering creek.

Lumber tycoons logged Sam's more mature trees and anticipated their own potential for becoming rich. But Sam, with always a step forward, was careful to arrange for his own needs. He contracted with the brokers and tycoons and dealers to have them fall the more lumber-rich trees and stockpile the lumber in exchange for finished lumber anytime Sam called for it. Sam controlled where the logger took out a tree. He had the logger take out a tree and clean up the underbrush in areas large enough for various sets of eventual farm buildings.

The woods in Sam Fisher's tract by the Pequea had sprung out of the richest of limestone soil. For centuries the trees had matured rapidly, weeded out naturally by lightning strike and left to rot, virtually free of storm damage, so that a tree designated for bridge planking was hardy and straight. *"The dream of the local mills!"*

Pequea Sam was able to foresee the demand for quality lumber for the settlements and for bridges to cross over the meandering Pequea Creek. He could see himself becoming rich and powerful without limit. "God calls man to heavy reckoning for overweening pride, and all arrogance will reap a harvest of tears," according to ancient Greek tragedy. The words meant nothing to the young "hustler" whose career was on a blindsided roll.

So it appeared destined for Sam, whose young life was becoming something of a Greek tragedy. As though his events were indeed determined by fates setting the stage, preordaining certain ill-fated events, with little left to the young man's choice.

Over the summer Pequea Sam's enterprise climbed steadily to an apex. For any ordinary man, life could not have become better. At the height of his wild success, however, Sam was thrown off track by his struggle between good and evil. Paramount was his ongoing struggle with hatred and unforgiveness. Thoughts about hating his unforgiving brother drove him to distraction.

"All is meaningless vanity. Everything under the sun is a meaningless vanity." He had read it in the Catacombs.

"You need to see a different kind of doctor," said the village doctor the day before. "You need one who can help you to see what's going on inside your head."

"Inside my head? Sounds like a some kind of witch doctor!"

⤐═ ═⤏

Pequea Sam came to the city looking for a real "head doctor. *"I'll find somebody, if it kills me,"* he told the trees and fences passing slowly outside of the trolley window.

Alas, the depression had followed so close behind that he was barely able to keep track of his own agenda. Sam walked the streets, disconnected from both himself and his fellowman. *"If I can not express myself on my own, how am I gonna open up to some strange head doctor?"*

"Sometimes life just has a way of going sour," said another head doctor, making Sam turn inside himself all the more. He tried staying to himself, but that became virtually impossible. So many were demanding so much of him that it would have been impossible to stay within himself. He tried "going with the flow," but at the same time he preferred to be off by himself.

People had been "milking" Sam for all he was worth. Most of them "took but did not give back." Others could not percieve the difference between taking or giving back. Ironically, the more people milked from the esteemed young man, the more they seemed to resent him. As though Envy, the green-eyed monster, was controlling them.

Sessions with the village therapist had stopped when Sam thought he was not getting the help he needed. It seemed like the therapist was only making matters worse. *"Last thing I need is to answer the man's self-serving questions that lead to nothing but a money relationship!"*

Fatigue set in. Sam was good for nothing except sitting under his meditation tree, struggling with good and evil. The young man appeared to be marching to the beat of some unknown drummer. He no longer wanted to be by himself in his shelter. He began to spend his evenings and overnights with the farmer and his family.

Chapter 7

The Madam

A troubled young man moved abruptly from beneath his meditation tree and headed for the trolley station. *"I feel competely worthless. I can longer hide the way I feel and am helpless to do anything about it! Since I can no longer change my situation, I am going to change myself. I'd better go look for a real 'head doctor' til I find one! There's gotta be a good one creeping around somewhere in this city!"*

Pequea Sam wandered aimlessly around the city. *"My life is turning sour real fast!"* Sam told himself. *"I'm starting to feel pretty much as though my life is shutting off, like I'm completely disconnected from everything and everybody that matters!"*

"Say, that looks like an very interesting place," the dejected young man finally told himself out loud. The front door was painted in a bright red. A red lamp sat boldly inside the window. It appeared like a friendly enough place with a soft, enticing red light. *"Now there's somebody who might make me feel better! I bet that would be just the place! Next time in the city I will check it out,"* he said, walking away from the gate.

"Suppose there is no next time?"

⊷⊨◯ ◯⊨⊷

The beaded curtain slid open. A bewhiskered Amish man stood beneath the red light, black hat in hand. The dolled-up lady looked intently at the bearded stranger, like she was staring right through him. At least that's what it felt like to Samuel. Bewildered by an endless "pregnant pause," he blurted the first words that entered his mind. *"I need to talk to somebody, anybody!"*

"Is that all you have in mind, coming in here just to talk to somebody, anybody?" the dolled-up lady parroted mockingly.

I need somebody who'll listen to what I have to say, <u>need</u> to say!

"Well, you've come to quite the wrong place! Know what a brothel is?"

"I guess so."

"No, you don't!"

"I've heard tell of a "house of ill fame." Is it that kind of place?"

"More or less. Ever hear of a *"fancy house?"* I prefer you talk of my place as such.

"Why fancy? Because it's got a red light?"

"That's but a small part of it."

"But all I want is somebody to listen!"

The fancy lady pondered the young Amish man closely but could not find words to raise to the next level of brothel talk.

"Come in."

The dolled up woman settled into her high-back chair surrounded by a sea of books in her lavish library. Normally she saw right through the men who came through her establishment. But this one she could not figure out. She observed the bearded stranger closely. To Samuel it felt like she was scrutinizing every hair in his red beard.

"Okay, so I'm listening. On with it."

Young Samuel clammed up at the deliberate and condescending approach. He fondled his black hat and fixed his stare upon the elaborate sea of books. When he raised his eyes, the dolled woman read a deep sorrow behind his imploring blue eyes.

No inner thrill greeted Samuel's new day – nothing left over from his visit to the fancy house the day before. Although he had come away with nothing, every thought was consumed with the house and its dolled-up proprietor.

Sam eased back into his nest, laced his fingers under his head, and stared into a million tiny red explosions fighting against the darkness, cursing his weakness for wishing he were still back at the "fancy house."

All day he wondered *why* he had ever stepped across the fancy lady's threshold in the first place. Curiosity? Pleasure? *"The place is, after all, a house of ill fame, a plain old house for harlots? I would not dare go back to such a place again!"*

Still Samuel remained ambivalent about going back for "just one more visit." He had so much to talk about and initially perceived the fancy house a safe enough place to begin to open up. He decided at length to give the fancy house another shot. *"I figure I'm safer opening up to the fancy lady, a lot safer than to two quack 'head doctors!' I need some place to vent freely, with emotion if need be. Something I have never done with my own tight-lipped people."*

Sam argued with himself. *"Suppose the fancy place would not be about therapy after all?"* He slipped back into bed and slept until past noon.

Early afternoon Sam woke up and decided he was going back to the city, hook or crook! He had already begun marching to the beat of a new drummer, however faint or distant the music. *"The trolley ride will do me good!"*

Once out of bed and set upon his mission, Sam felt led by the nose. His first stop after crossing over the trolley tracks was at the People's Apothecary on Penn Square to buy a cigar. *"To enhance my image?"*

He walked down Queen Street, the main road heading south, still battling over a second visit to the fancy house. With no particular destination in mind, he stopped off at Joe's Bar for a quick snort. *"Courage for the times?"*

--==○   ○==--

On Sam's second visit, the fancy lady met him in her garden. "As you shall see, I am mighty proud of my garden!" A famous Greek philosopher once said that *he who has a garden and a library wants for nothing!* "Same goes for *my own* library and beloved garden!"!

The fancy lady "counseled" Sam while she moved among her exotic flowers, occasionally whiffing at a new bud and casually pruning shoots. "Flowers are my music! They have no emotions and therefore no conflicts." She breathed life into the buds by talking to the more "weary" ones. "See what happens to the flower after it is cut off from its life-giving source?"

Now and then she brushed up against her "prospective client," casually stealing a buss from a cheek or giving his red whiskers an affectionate tug.

"I kinda go for this lady's 'casual ordinariness'!"

Outside Joe's Bar, after a few "short snorts," Sam was suddenly visited with a new low. His lows always followed the same pattern. First, by the same old curse over stealing the *blessing of the forefathers*, followed with feeling sorry over his "humble beginning." Sam constantly wrestled with being bugged or guilt-ridden over *something.* Tonight would be no exception.

"Jacob has no cause ever to forgive me! Not ever!"

--==○   ○==--

What should have been his third visit, Samuel flat-out snubbed the fancy lady. He ambled aimlessly past her house on the way back to the trolley station, then home to find solace at the foot of his "meditation tree." There he decided to stay out of the city and give one of the local "quacks" another go. However he suddenly grew afraid to confide in *anyone* about the things going on in his life.

Tonight he had actually looked forward to opening up to the dolled-up lady, but then in his confusion thought it much too absurd to place his confidence in a brothel madam, of all people!

"I prefer to keep matters as they are, and not bring up Jacob to anybody!"

⊶⊶ ⊷⊷

"You worship success, don't you, Sam? You belong to a culture where everything is geared in terms of success, measured by money," the madam pointed out during Sam's third visit. "You allow success to go to your head! It's like being a success has become a religion with you!"

Surely you have run across people who don't want others to be what they are not willing to be themselves. That applies directly to your type. Your so-called *religion* has no life; that's why it's so oppressive!"

Truth or not, Sam was hurt by the madam's blunt approach. Seated under the "meditation tree," he suddenly wished to go back into the Catacombs. *"There my spirit had life. Only now some brothel madam makes like she wants to kick me out!"* We were taught in *Das Alte Landt* to stick with *Freunde,* not just up and kick up a fuss if something or somebody didn't suit us, or if we disagreed over something.

The dreaded "down spirals" kept on making the young man's life more frightening and unpredictable. *"I just hafta risk opening up to somebody, anybody! So why don't I give the dolled up lady and her fancy place just one last crack!"*

"Sam, I may just be a typical brothel madam, but I care enough to say this to you anyhow. You *have* to stop looking so sad all the time. Your sadness makes my spirit heavy as well. I sense that you are dragging me down with you! Happiness is like a butterfly, ya know. The more you chase it, the more it will elude you. But if you turn your attention to other things, it comes and softly sits on your shoulder!"

After the visit, their fourth, Sam decided he that he may have found a *special* kind of therapy after all, the help he needed and was looking for. The fancy lady's soft demeanor threatened to break down some of the stoicism that Pequea Sam that had been dragging along with himself, all the way from the *Das Alte Landt* to inside some fancy brothel!

However slowly, Sam started to trust the dolled-up lady to listen, without judging her or without fear that she may have been betraying his confidence. He was also learning, however slowly, the value in opening up about the pain he was feeling.

By the end of several more visits, the young man's pain started to pour forth more readily. The chief cause of his depression – being disconnected from self and others – was slowly beginning to erode. "You don't have to tell me *anything* more about yourself. It's written all over your countenance!"

Chapter 8

Yolanda

Her christened name was Yolanda. She was once a dedicated *hausfrau* and a faithful woman in the Quaker church. But over time, trying circumstances kept coming down on her and her marriage began to go sour. She began to spend less time with her family and longed for more free time.

Liz ran an "escort service." They offered her a "position" and she grabbed it. "Great! at last I am going be that career person I've always deserved to be! I will *buy* the independence I've been wanting for such a long time!"

Before long, Yolanda found the "position" with the escort service repulsive. However, the pay was so good and the temptation for money so great, that she gave to the position all she had anyway. She "performed her duties" so diligently that Liz designated her a *madam*. In turn as Liz's madam, Yolanda continually ran such a clean ship for Liz and made so much money, that she ended up with her own "fancy house."

Yolanda's "power" came from the powerful silence she had experienced at the Quaker meetings. Not from any personal faith, but from her own will power, like one who considered herself with the same power as a *braucher*. The same spiritual awareness Yolanda recalled feeling in her Quaker church, where she had found power by meditating in silence, was the same warmth she often felt now.

At one time in Yolanda's past, she considered herself a virtuous woman, in spite of the way she made her "living." Unfortunately, she would be "defined" by her profession. "If Sam Fisher is the man he professes to be, why should he care anything about some common brothel madam?"

Yolanda was what she referred to as a "proprietor of a brothel, a/k/a as a fancy house." There had once been a shadow side to her. She had made love with reckless abandon and led many an innocent man down the dangerous road of obsessive love or of loveless, manipulative sex. She had been a seducer and a thief of innocence to many young men. Too often they had to learn their lessons the hard way.

However Yolanda now occupied herself in pursuits other than the mere running of a house of ill fame. Her soothing voice and pleasant demeanor eventually made her much more than the common "proprietor of a brothel." Her ordinariness made her extraordinary and attracted her "prospective young client" far more than did any mind doctor he had encountered. *"I think she is the very person I can trust enough to put my faith into!"*

"Ya know, sometimes I have to do *some* things worthwhile, something good and right, lest my Creator strike me down!" Inclined to his own brand of self-righteousness, Sam headed for the trolley station, left hanging by the madam's surprising last statement.

"Why should the Creator care a measly bit about how somebody runs a brothel, anyhow?"

The day Sam Fisher admitted he needed help, the dawn for him broke like a new, refreshing day. The fancy house was like a new day dawning, an undefinable new chapter. *"Like the day I decided to gave up the hunger strike and finally began accepting food from Chaplain Visser!"*

He became excited beyond measure when the fancy lady first hinted about addressing her as "madam." At the thought, his personality erected to its compelling, magnetic self, the way it did in the Catacombs on occasion. Immediately the floodgates opened for Sam, and the things he spoke about caused the fancy lady's mind to be erected in turn.

"Poppycock!" the lady exclaimed after observing the normally shy Sam as he expounded about himself and his past. Among other things, "introduced" his twin brother Jacob for the first time, about the *Blessing of the Fathers,* even about how the "botched up blessing" had turned into a generational curse, tainting their very flesh and blood.

"*I carry a heavy agenda: my brother's vindication!*"

"Poppycock, really now?"

With all the fancy lady had heard, she began to carry a heavy agenda as well -- the well-being of her "man." She found herself "rediscovering God" in the process of mentoring Sam and romanticized how it once was back in the Quaker church. For the first time, she sensed a "professional" relationship to be gained for herself, something far more than mere sex-for-hire or occasional money. Above all, she wanted justice for her man. However, she would face obstacles on every turn -- everything and everybody!

"This is indeed my man! With his help I shall find my way back to the way I once was. He will take me back to my roots!" For the dolled-up lady, at first blush it appeared too good to be true. But then it fit with everything else that had been happening for the two of them.

Sam tried hard to perform for the brothel owner in a predictable manner, ever so careful to put on his best face, so that his behavior became virtually "prescribed." At one session he carried a happy demeanor; at another he refused to make even eye contact with his "advisor," like he was ashamed to be in her presence.

Sam thought that the brothel madam could not detect his mood change. However, she easily picked up on it and always had a way to deal with it. She was sharp and discerning that way. It's what made her a good proprietor and at the same time a meaningful counselor!

⊷═◉ ◉═⊷

Sam was at all times preoccupied with mending things with Jacob. *"I cannot imagine that God in His mercy would do anything other than to bring us together!"*

Being together in the New World would afford the brothers an opportunity to make things right, maybe even to reconcile. Sam would have wanted nothing more. *"Yet I constantly wrestle with how much Jacob must hate me! How do I handle my brother's wrath? I agonize over how desperately both of us need peace of mind and body!"*

At times Sam imagined the two brothers reuniting and starting out with a clean slate, so that one day he would at last be vindicated from Jacob's wrath! Still he sensed his faith becoming feeble from wrestling over what the Fates said would have to be, saved only by his mantra: *"Behold the turtle. He makes progress only when he sticks his neck out !"*

After Sam had finished spilling his heart about his brother, he felt better about himself. Moreover, he felt especially good after his last several visits with the lady. His *visits* had now become *sessions* with her behest about going to see her regularly. "You will be my *client*, Sam Fisher. And you shall address me as *Madam*."

Samuel had just found a heightened self-esteem and a new freedom that catapulted him to sudden success within the settlement. The 500-acre grant on the Pequea *exuded* prosperity!

"Some folks are even starting to refer to me as Pequea Sam!"

⊷═◉ ◉═⊷

Pequea Sam regularly confided in his madam about the despair he felt over the unfinished business with his brother Jacob.

"Everybody make mistakes in life," the madam stressed to her client. "But that doesn't mean they should have to pay for them for the rest of their life. Sometimes good people make bad choices, but that doesn't they're *bad*. It simply means they're human. They say that worry is like a rocking chair. It gives you something to do, but it doesn't get you anywhere. It's all-important to remember that joy always comes on the heels of despair, provided we don't cave in!"

In time, however, Sam had difficulty opening up about his brother to his madam. He'd been leaving her fancy house physically drained. "Your well has been stuffed up with dirt," the madam said. "A bit of levity would unstop it."

"Not anything could lighten me up right now."

"Sometimes I simply do not know how to live with myself, Madam."

"Yo, then this session has got to be about *you!* "There has got to be a reason why you're telling me that you don't like yourself, Pequea Sam. Underneath the topmost layers of frailty, a man wants to feel good about himself, and to be loved. Because when he comes to die – no matter what his influence or talent or genius – if he dies unloved, his life will be a failure to him and his dying a cold horror! We humans are constantly entangled in questions of good and evil. It's the only story we know. There is no other story. In the end, no matter who or what we are, we all seek the same answers. A man, after brushing off the dust and chips in his life, will face only the clean, hard questions. *Was I loved or was I hated? Was my life good or was it evil? Did I do good or did I do ill? Will my life be a loss, or will some joy come from it?*

No worry, Sam. I meant to say that worry is like sitting in a rocking chair. It gives you something to do, but it doesn't get you anywhere. I'm not working to get you to feel any better about yourself. Just to get you to love the person you already are.

"First off, we are not given a *good* life or a *bad* life. We are simply given <u>life</u>*!* It's up to us to make it good or bad! Furthermore, you are not necessarily a product of your circumstances. You are a product of your *decisions.* How often do we pray, 'Master, forgive us our debts as we forgive our debtors?' You must simply *decide* to forgive your brother, Sam. In turn the Master will forgive *you!*"

For a long while they sat without talking. The madam could tell that her client was troubled. So she decided just to love her man and to *hope* that he would eventually come to love *himself.* By the same token, the madam is destined to rediscover *herself* in the process of mentoring her man.

It had been a rather lengthy session, a lot of it without talking. The chief cause of Pequea Sam's depression, being disconnected from self and others, was beginning to erode. By the end of the session, he decided that last he had found the help he had been seeking from any of his so-called "head doctors."

His madam's soft demeanor had been breaking down the stoicism he had brought with him to her place. *"I am learning the value in speaking up about how I feel, Madam. I trust you to listen without betraying my confidence!"*

⊷⟾ ⟾⊶

At Joe's Bar, Pequea Sam pondered his madam's rather lengthy session. *"One thing sure, my madam has my best interest at heart. On the other hand, would the madam be siding with my brother if <u>he</u> were the one who'd been coming to <u>her</u> for advice? How could I ever stoop so low as to give out the deepest secrets of my heart to some brothel madam? That's the last thing I <u>ever</u> wanted to do!"*

Approaching the trolley station, the esteemed Pequea Sam appeared a lonely and afflicted man. He stopped by the side of the road, motionless save for the gentle swaggering of the body – head down, eyes all but closed, hands shoved deep into his pockets --as he sang a muffled *"O Happy Day that fixed my choice...."*

That said it all. Sung by one who was physically spent and on the verge of spiritually bankruptcy!

⊷⇒ ⇐⊶

Pequea Sam was becoming more and more performance-driven. No one except his madam knew what drove him and kept him going. The church wags had decided he was motivated by the desire for esteem within his church district. The wags further decided that as a new member of the community and congregation, he was seeking to achieve favor by succeeding in a land where so many had been struggling with the elements.

When things were on the upbeat, then life abounded for Pequea Sam. The youthful pioneer was slowly learning how to turn every burst of energy into the dream he had for his brother Jacob.

During his upswings, his boundless energy and enthusiasm carried him as though on eagle's wings. During his downers, however, he was unpredictable and fierce, thinking it was needful to go off by himself for as long it took to stabilize. *"I'll sit under my "meditation tree," then walk to the village to see what's up with my English buddies."* On the other hand, the time he spent with his village buddies always ended the same way. He often despised himself for not making better use of his time, then gave himself over to heavy toil.

Pequea Sam's new building venture also included a more formal church gathering, in which a small group of volunteers laid out the skeleton of a house on the ground. Parts of the crew came along sometime later to prepare the forms for "raising the house." With plans and frames and people in place, the actual construction went off like clockwork under the quiet leadership of the "ball of energy" who had recently emigrated from the Old Country.

The new venture thrived with the help of newly-made friends and with those fellow church members who regularly showed up to help. Whatever the reason, Pequea Sam Fisher prospered immensely, despite the significant chink in his armor – those highs and lows he so successfully kept hidden.

⊷⊜ ⊜⊶

In one final session with his madam, Pequea Sam threw one more pressing question at her. *"Do you think my brother (ever) loved me?"*

"Jacob hated even himself! He spread his hatred around like butter on hot bread. I've heard it said that the acid of hate destroys the container! Some people come into your life as blessings; others comes into your life as lessons!" said his madam.

"So once and for all, put aside the question of caring whether or not your brother ever loved you and to go about the business of being human, of loving others. For in so doing, your brother may eventually learn to love *himself!*"

⊷⊜ ⊜⊶

"Write to your brother, Samuel. *You must be first. But just do it!* Let Jacob *feel* like you love him, which I know you do. Be careful to use the right words as you approach him after those years. In short, you might first have to help him love *himself!* Bear this in mind, Samuel. By now your brother might have decided that he flat-out hates you!"

"It's been a lot of years you know! Don't be surprised if he ignores you, no matter your approach. Make sure that every word you use on your long-lost brother is like a "favor." Like a *gift,* freely given by your grace, out of a loving heart!"

"Moreover, no gift will ever *buy back* a man's love when he feels you have removed his *self*-love. Once a word is uttered, it's uttered. You can't change it. We can say *"sorry"* over and over, but still it has been uttered! The word is *powerful.* You do it first, Samuel; don't wait for your brother."

It had been a grueling session for Pequea Sam, starting with a rather simple yet straightforward question about loving and being loved, later with thoughts dominated by his madam. With all that was accomplished, Sam walked out with greater conviction – chin up, face straight ahead. Every tree looked greener as the trolley slowly headed back out of the city.

Jacob's hoped-for arrival sparked a new surge in prosperity under the madam, giving Pequea Sam a new lease in life and a sense of well-being that mounted him on eagle's wings. *"I will live in my humble hogan and build Jacob's family a house of many rooms! I'll even shelter his livestock!"*

Once again the young prisoner from the Catacombs appeared preordained for another surge in prosperity, spurred by the hope that Jacob would respond favorably to his letter and decide to become part of his estranged brother's new world in the Pequea.

No sooner was Sam's letter on the way to the Old Country than he agonized over whether Jacob and his family would indeed come to the New World, much less answer his letter. *"What will we discover when they do come after all this time?"* Every morning before digging into his work, he stopped at the "meditation tree" to deal with the agony of not knowing.

Sometime during the next session with his madam, Sam rather casually brought up the latest concerning his brother Jacob, but then abruptly clammed up. *"I don't wish to discuss any matters with Jacob with you again!"*

"When a man says he does not want to speak about something, it usually means he can think of nothing else. As justified as your brother may feel in his desire for vengeance, he may never get a penny's worth of justice. And if he does, will it ever be enough?"

"Oh, but I love my brother. Maybe he is not what I wish him to be as far as forgiveness is concerned. But I'm not a perfect person either! I make a lot of mistakes. I appreciate those people deeply who decide to stick with me even after knowing how I really am!"

"Granted, it takes two to tango! And it works both ways. However, you are much too anxious over things that are beyond your control. You don't know whether your brother even *wants* to leave the Old Country. Likely he's comfortable just staying there!"

"He'll come. He simply must come! Otherwise, how can we finish our business? It's the Master's business too, you know. On the other hand, I'm afraid of what may happen when we <u>do</u> see each other!"

The madam was aware of her client's deep angst and felt a helpless compassion for her man. "Just forgive your brother from the heart, then let the Master do the rest."

When Jacob did not respond to Sam's letter, all sorts of ironic twists began to unleash. First of all, he suffered rejection and fell into a deep funk, like he saw his father do when he virtually died in life over the hopelessness he had experienced with the tainting of the *Blessing*. Now Samuel was taking on the same symptoms, because he was not able to reunite with his brother. He took sick, just like he had seen his father do. However, the madam thought Samuel was just having another bout with depression.

"You feel rejected because your brother hasn't answered your letter. What did you expect? Do you know that rejection usually comes from those who matter the most to us; and who matters more to you than Jacob, the one whose heel you had grabbed at birth?"

"Most likely your brother is still holding onto old anger that came from rejection, the same as you, and does not know *how* to forgive because no one ever taught him how! It would be an insult to the glory of his anger to forgive you!"

"Shuck off the dead weight of anger over not hearing. Holding on it may be what's been bringing you all this remorse! I've heard it said that nothing is so sad as an association trying to hold together by the glue of a postage stamp. If you can't see or touch a man, don't you think it's better just to let him go?

"No matter what you do for your brother, for one who is so vindictive, is it ever going to be enough? They say that a man can die and the nation ring with praise for what he was; when just beneath it rings with gladness that he is dead. There's nothing more you *can* do. You can't spend the rest of your natural life hoping to undo something that's already over with. It's over, Pequea Sam! Dead. How long will you kick a dead horse in the ribs?"

"You know Madam, I guess when it comes right down to it, I never did like my brother!"

"Don't hate, Sam! Hatred only stirs up strife. Please don't even mention the *hatred* word again! It's *love* that covers a multitude of sins, you know. The mere mention of hating someone or something can virtually shrivel your soul. To repeat – if your brother does you wrong, rebuke him; and if he repents, then forgive him!"

⁘⟺ ⟺⁘

The madam was an ardent tea drinker, concocting her own, using a variety of fruit, flower and plant. When she began making "tea" just for Sam, she could be seen, stealthily as a witch, creeping about in the early morning, silently gathering weeds and herbs. Making tea for Sam had become an obsession.

"Whatever it takes to keep my man well!"

As the madam gave up her own spirit for "her man," a new man gradually emerged in Pequea Sam. The pains of prior rejection had all but disappeared. With this new wholeness, Sam Fisher increased in the eyes of the community rather than withdrawing from everybody, even from Big Heart, his trusted friend. He emerged with an increased hope and a new life as the sessions with his madam had become a regular thing. Eventually, Sam carried a new *spirituality* back to his "Church in the Colony."

At the same time there emerged a different woman in Sam's madam! Here was a fiercely self-reliant woman, a brothel proprietor, who had once lived for pleasure alone. Earlier on, she had made a choice to compromise bed and family and fortune – even happiness – to create a world to fit her carefully-created and private universe. Here was a woman so self-centered that her world seemed to revolve solely around her.

Once there had been a shadow side to the madam. She had made love with reckless abandon and had led many an innocent man down the dangerous road of obsessive love or of loveless, manipulative sex. She had become known among men as a seducer, a thief of innocence to many a young man. She was exceptionally skilled at leading the innocent and wide-eyed young man by the nose. In turn she could hang him out to dry, leaving him to learn some of his lessons the hard way.

Later, as Head Madam, she boasted of being a sexual *Mentor*. As such it was her function to *initiate* her men into the mysteries of love or sex, someone she referred as a sexual *initiator*, a partner who helped her men experience the power of sex as a vehicle of higher consciousness. She boasted of going so far as to actually leading her lover "to experience the divine!"

⊷═◉ ◉═⊷

One day the Head Madam declared it was high time to make some drastic changes! Many a times Pequea Sam caught her off in a daze, trying to deal with her past. From thirsting from guilt, from regret, from nights of making love to countless lonely men and finding no love. "Prayer does not necessarily 'change things' as the saying goes. Prayer actually changes *me,* so then I will be free to change things!"

In time there developed a co-dependency between the brothel madam and her *client* Sam Fisher. Two needy people – one with a need for love; the other with a need to administer "tender loving care." Each was feeding off the other to form an addictive relationship, an addiction made all the more enticing by their secret trysts.

Pequea Sam thrived on his madam's encouragement. So much that now and then, when he was in the middle of an "upper," he envisioned his own "Amish empire" of sorts, with his madam as co-founder and beneficiary.

⊷═◉ ◉═⊷

"You can't measure your worth by the way somebody else treats you. You work hard to love and *be* loved, but you appear to lose the joy that comes with it. Sometimes you forget just how to laugh! Maybe your well is stuffed up with dirt. A little laughter would go a long way to unstop it. The devil is having you for lunch, messing with your peace, stealing your joy!"

The madam looked her client squarely in the face. "This is not the end of the world, you know. Nothing is the end of the world except the end of the world, so don't give up! Take control of your destiny! Believe in yourself. Ignore those who try to discourage you. Avoid negative sources, people, places, things and habits!"

"As justified as your brother may be in his desire for vengeance, he may never get a penny's worth of justice. And if he does, will it ever be enough?"

"Maybe not. But I'm certainly not giving up!"

⊷══◉ ◉══⊶

Every week Pequea Sam caught the trolley to visit his madam in the city, something he considered a valuable utilization of his time. No one questioned where he went when they observed him cross the trolley tracks. No one thought twice what he did while he was gone, only that he always seemed rejuvenated.

Sam Fisher was proud of his farmground. With every acre made tillable he felt good about what he himself was becoming -- powerful and in control, like one soaring on eagles' wings. So long as the the young visionary could perform in this fashion, his crippling malady of manic depression would go unnoticed, so that with time the spiritual and industrious young man fought successfully against both element and savage.

At all times, Sam was jealous of his personal image. Seems he was born with had an innate need to be successful and respected. It was difficult enough to be both successful and respected in the Colony. But Pequea Sam managed both and still to be let alone to follow his pursuits, despite the propensity in the Colony for busybodyness. *"It should not be any concern of theirs anyhow, seeing as how I always return normal and get back to my work!"*

⊷══◉ ◉══⊶

In the New World, Pequea Sam was held in high esteem in the church community. He kept opinions to himself and appeared confident in church matters, a self-confidence that carried him on wings. As time wore on, however, he realized he was looking at the situation with his madam through rose-colored glasses. This only heightened his inner conflict as new fears crowded his imagination.

His "Amish empire" would crumble like a house of matchsticks if he and the madam were ever found out. His self-righteous church friends would turn an about-face and go their own way. Same with the law-abiding neighbors, who decided they could not love such a neighbor as themselves.

In time, it became more and more difficult for the young man to juggle loyalties between church elders and civic leaders. He feared what would happen if he and his madam were found out.

"Would one or the other faction acknowledge her as a spiritual counselor? Or would both of them look down their noses and simply consider her a common proprietor of a brothel?" Certain grave consequences were bound to come on the heels of the latter! The spiritually sensitive man would not be able to handle such a crisis.

⊷⇒ ⇐⊶

Meanwhile in *Das Alte Landt,* Jacob was seriously contemplating a move to the New World after Sam had invited him so many times. However in the midst of preparing himself and his family to go, Jacob became ordained by lot to serve his congregation as their preacher. This prompted Jacob to feel that now he would be all the more entitled to the *Blessing of the Fathers.* In turn, that heaped all the more guilt and hopelessness upon Sam!

Jacob decided to go forward with the move and to heed his call to go serve as a preacher somewhere within the Pequea District. Rather than staying in the Old Country, he would simply transfer his calling to the New World and serve in his brother's congregation in the Upper Pequea District.

Jacob said he was taking a blind leap of faith into the unknown when he decided to go to the New World. He had made no promises. Said he would was going for *"the sake of the Church and for no other reason!"* However, by saying this and in that manner it appeared that Jacob was not fully ready to give up the hatred for his brother Samuel.

Then Jacob learned of the madam to boot!

On some mornings, before digging into his work, Pequea Sam served his double-mindedness by leaving his perch under the tree and walking through the woods to the village to spend time with his English buddies. *"I have got to occupy my mind with lighter things to keep from falling apart entirely!"*

Chapter 9

Father Jacob's New World

With Jacob and his wife Annie in tow came their precocious ten-year-old Samuel. They called him Little Sammy from the day he was born, being the second Samuel Fisher in the recent Fisher family tree. The moniker stuck because he reminded everybody of his uncle, Samuel Fisher. Little Sammy had been destined to rise to a rapid maturity. First it by living on a cargo ship, then it was by living among the Native American people. Then combined with his many people skills, and finally by riding it out with his many and varied human triangles.

Sammy II

When I got to be a little older, I was "Sammy the Younger" and then finally "Sammy II." I shall remember as long as I live how that when my uncle lived in the Old Country how I faithfully trotted at his heels and followed him everywhere. "Little heeltrotter," my uncle would call me affectionately.

Uncle Sam doted on me like the son he never had. "Lucky the father who has a son the likes of you," my uncle quipped, tousling my forever strubbled bangs and tossing me into the air. I adored Uncle Sam, always eager to have him toss me high as he could, not the least anxious whether he might miss me coming down!

"I love Uncle Sam, he is my goodest best friend!" I said it as long as I can remember, and to this day I still can not imagine anything better to than to grow up in the shadow of such a hero. I did everything in my power just to please the man. I forever wanted to remain a boy and be doted on by Uncle! -

Alas, one day my Uncle Sam disappeared like a puff of smoke! Mother had been shielding me from him whenever he was around and barely let me speak to him. "Your Uncle Sam is an evil man," she said after he disappeared.

I barely understood the meaning of crime and evil. I only knew the memory of Uncle Sam and the gentle rough-housing. I chose to remember nothing else.

One day someone leaked the cruelest rumor and it spread like a house afire. They said that Uncle Sam was put somewhere in a prison. My heart broke into a million pieces and ached with disbelief and a homesickness. Day after day I longed for the one who had forever been my idol.

⋆⟾ ⟻⋆

The day Father Jacob told us that we got a letter from Uncle Sam was like a great new day dawning. I was beside myself and pined to know my beloved uncle as I once had. All the good things I remembered about him crowded into my mind at once and kept me excited every waking moment. All day long I daydreamed of seeing my uncle and never again letting him get out of my sight!

It was a happy time when Mother and Father stopped bickering all the time, with Mother talking loud all the time, and Father Jacob not saying nothing. *"At least now I know what most of fuss was about. They were trying to keep a secret from me after they first got Uncle's letter!"*

My heart stopped beating when Father Jacob told us that Uncle Sam had been living in the New World and had sent word for us to come and visit him there, maybe even to live over there. And now I knew what the other half of their argument had been. It was about *settling* in the New World, whatever that meant. *"All I care to know is that Uncle Sam had arranged with a missionary from the New World for us to go across the Big Water in a cargo ship. Father would be a deck hand and Mother would be the cook's helper!"*

All I *really* cared about was that my uncle was the stuff of my dreams; and about how much I wanted to be around him once again!

⋇⟾ ⟻⋇

Mother did not want to go and live in the New World and leave her beloved people behind. So she took it out on all of us – on Father one day and me the next. It seemed like me and Father had a secret pact to stick together and not cave in. The more she raved and ranted, the more eager Father was to see the New World and me to see my beloved uncle. Father never said much, and that set Mother off all the more.

We were a mess by the time we got across the Big Water, with Mother grumbling all the way and pretending to be sick much of the time. *"I reckon she just didn't want to be the cook's helper. I could tell right away when she glared at the cook that they weren't going to hit it off!"*

Whenever Father Jacob wasn't working, he would go off by himself. He always looked to me like he was in deep thought. *"It looks like something is really bothering my father!"*

By the time we saw the "promised land" way off in the distance, we were all done in. No one was arguing about much of anything or mad at anyone, because we were all so done in.

⋇⟾ ⟻⋇

After Jacob Fisher finally agreed to move himself and his family from *Das Alte Landt* to the New World, he did it at his brother Sam's bidding. He had finally decided that he would leave the Old Country with one driving force -- to *"get away from the devil!"*

From the beginning his road was rough. It took a tough man to travel it, and Jacob was the one who could do it. He was a stern man coming into a stern age, and into a rough and violent country.

Jacob Fisher's church life had not been simple in the Old Country. He was deeply concerned with rules-keeping, which kept him steeped in legalism – an "ism" exulting rules over relationship. He believed that abiding by the *Ordnung* (rules of the district) was paramount and would earn himself a place, or at the very least, eternal points in the *Kingdom*. But to Jacob Fisher the church lived and died by the rules of the *Ordnung*.

Yet Jacob remained passionate in his hatred toward his own brother.

-->==◎ ◎==<--

Jacob Fisher professed to "put on the whole armor of God" but had plenty chinks in his armor. First off, he was crippled by guilt, which was making the young man old before his time. Secondly, his remorse robbed him of energy and kept him physically and mentally out of kilter much of the time. The remorse made it difficult to be open with the folks with whom it was so necessary to relate.

More than anything, the young preacher needed emotional healing from hatred and unforgiveness. His stoicism made his battles with forgiveness an especially formidable task. He believed when it came time to forgive his brother, forgiving would be a matter he could handle on his own. But to him, *forgetting* would become an altogether different matter. Lack of faith in a Higher

Power had been the essence of the young man's struggle, and with that he struggled every waking moment.

"Of course I forgive my brother! I forgave him a long time ago. Who would I think I am *not* to forgive him? Besides, if I don't forgive, then the Lord will not forgive me either! A wise writer once said that he who cannot forgive another, will break the bridge over which he must one day pass himself!"

Forgetting was for young Jacob an altogether different matter! It was far easier for the legalistic young preacher to utter the "forgiveness" word with his lips than to practice it in his heart.

No matter the extent of his effort, or the extent of his struggle, Jacob could not let go of how gravely his own flesh and blood had wronged him. Stealing the blessing of the forefathers was to Jacob a blasphemy against the Holy Ghost and was unpardonable. Hating Sam had become for Jacob an inner vow he thought he had to live and abide by.

Most tragic of all was that Jacob did not believe he was hurting anyone!

⇥⇒ ⇐⇤

At our landing place at the mouth of the Delaware River, we met two peculiar-looking fellows with a reddish skin color. They wore brightly-colored bands around their heads and large feathers sticking up out of the bands. The two had been directed by an Indian leader to take us to "the man with the red beard."

"Uncle Sam? I just knew it!"

We carried ourselves and our belongings down out from the cargo ship and placed them into two large canoes. As the two reddish men paddled away from the landing place, I noticed that one of them spoke good English.

"This is called 'The Mouth of the Delaware'. A much bigger river, the Susquehanna, named by the Susquehannocks, empties into it out of the north. We will paddle our canoes up the big river to where it is joined by a creek, called the "Pequea." The Pequea Creek is named for our Pequea brothers. There we will find our leader. Our leader will then direct us to your landing spot."

All afternoon we paddled up the long, winding creek called the Pequea. "I come from the friendly tribe called *the Lenape.* Your brother calls me Big Heart," a muscular Indian told Father Jacob.

Big Heart paddled a bit farther and then led us toward a large clearing. Inside the clearing was a round house with a tool shed beside it. *"Is that where my uncle lives?"*

"Yep, that is your uncle's house, Sonny Boy. Now and then he goes away. Sometimes he stays away for several days," said the big Indian who could read the worry on our faces. "But he always comes back. That is his home after all, wait for him there."

My thoughts rose and fell like the paddle as we came into the clearing. I tingled inside my skin with every splash. But after no one was there to meet us, my heart suddenly felt heavy. Mother strutted around with her hands on her hips. "Now don't this beat all? Does your brother even *know* that we are here? Well, he ain't even here!" she exclaimed, lighting into Father Jacob.

With all the fuss around us, I did not notice the boy with the large feathers off in the woods a few paces from where we were standing. The young Indian lad watched -- wide-eyed and curious -- as the people dressed in black walked into the white man's barn.

Little Big Heart

When the boy from the Old Country met the Indian boy from the New World, it was love at first sight. Sammy II was gaga over the energetic Native American boy, who was just as fascinated with the wide-eyed, shy stranger with the blond bangs hanging in his eyes. "My father is the stranger's friend and helps him work around his new farm," said the feathered boy in unsteady English. "And the stranger calls my father 'Grosse Hertz' or 'Big Heart'."

"Hey, that would be my Uncle Sam! My father named me *Samuel,* for my uncle! That's why they call me *Sammy II.*

"And I am Big Heart's son. That's why some of the white folks call me *Little Big Heart!*

From the outset, Annie did not approve of her Sammy II hanging around the "young savage." She vehemently insisted that the two boys were not to play together. However, from their first meeting they had already formed a "mutual admiration society of two." Despite the mother's objection, a close and enduring friendship was already beginning, and boy with feathers in his hair and the one with bangs in his eyes, always managed to find each other.

⋆⇒⇐⋆

Me and Mother sat in the barn with the stuff we brought along with us across the Big Water. Nobody was saying anything, and I was all nervous that Uncle Sam wasn't there. Father came back to the shed looking lost. His eyes were fixed on the floor of the shed forebay. Mother kept shooting his mistakes at him, as if everything unexplainable was somehow his fault.

I felt bad for Father Jacob, the family leader and soon to be living in a New World. I quietly watched him fall apart. First over Uncle Sam not being here to meet us, and then over Mother lighting into him. *"I bet he don't even know we're here!"* said Mother condescendingly.

Things weren't going "right" or as he had hoped in they would go for him in the New World. I suppose he often "romanticized" the good life he was leaving behind back in the Old Country.

Uncle Sam's dappled gray horse whinnied from his pen off to the side. He schnobbled at my hand and rubbed his shoulder hard against the stall gate, no doubt begging to be let out. *"I think the horse wants to be let out."*

"No doubt he does."

"What do you think its name is?" I asked Father to relax him a bit.

"I guess it must be *Smokey*, judging from the color of his fur?"

"I bet it's a Barney. Everybody family needs to have just one Barney." Father chuckled at the meaningless conclusion.

⊷⇒ ⇐⊷

Mother was off somewhere looking into the wooden teepee they called a hogan. I fastened a neck rope to Barney's halter and led him down a familiar path to a large tree and back again. *"Can I hitch Barney to the wagon and drive him around a little bit?"*

The wagon was shaped like a big box on wheels. The wheels wobbled fiercely, like the wooden spokes needed binding. The wagon was rectangular, with a backless seat that was fastened to the floor. About a foot deep. Big wooden wheels with yellow spokes bound by a steel rim. The back end had an end gate. You can let it flop open if there was nothing in the wagon to slide off. Two could sit at the endgate and let their legs dangle over the end. On the very front of the wagon was a board called "a mud splasher" to keep running hoofs from throwing up stones and gravel into the buggy box.

Me and Barney clip-clopped down a well-worn lane to where it met up with a larger road, then turned around and headed back to the shed. "The woods are lovely and deep, my Father. Jump on and

I'll take you out the lane and back." My father clambered eagerly up over the wobbly yellow wheel.

Father Jacob was cheerful as we drove into Uncle Sam's deep, lovely woods. "Take a gee here," his chin instructed as we came upon the big road. "See where this goes."

We clip-a-clopped down the gravelly road, enjoying the new freedom from the lifeless cargo ship. Me and Father savored the gentle wind from the New World, laughing and not knowing where we were going nor what we were even looking for. Barney was happy and so were we, on this our first day on the soil of the New World.

"Someone comes, my son," said Father Jacob about a lone figure walking in our direction. The man's head was bent forward, as if lost in a world off by himself. He was walking very slowly, and appeared to be deeply in thought.

Siblings

Two long-lost siblings--one slight and fair-haired, the other large and swarthy--stood face to face on the road leading in from the village, like Fate had suddenly thrust them into each other's hands. The siblings froze in place, each one examining the other long and hard. Like a Mexican Standoff, where the weaker one flinches and gives away the store! My father gave in first.

Father Jacob vaulted over the wagon wheel and ran up to Uncle Sam, like he was about to embrace him. But Uncle Sam was already lying on the ground. My father knelt down and lifted Uncle Sam up from the gravel.

Nobody said anything. They just knelt there with their faces toward each other, like they were still examining each other.

Emotions ran to the core, so deep that neither could have even uttered the first word.

I stayed on the wagon and tingled all the way to the roots of my hair over suddenly being this close to my Uncle Sam! I had grown since the last time we have seen each other, enough to realize that I was a little too big to toss in the air anymore. But just touching my uncle would have been fine. This wasn't meant to be my moment.

The brothers stood up from the gravel. After Father Jacob helped Uncle Sam onto the end gate, I drove Barney back to the shed. "We will sleep in your barn, like we did last night," said Father Jacob, beating my uncle to the draw.

"No no, Jacob, you will sleep in your *very own* house," said Uncle Sam, pointing down the logging path to the gee side of the gravel lane.

"But the barn will be plenty good," repeated Father Jacob.

Uncle Sam turned and faced my father on the end gate, as if there was nothing more to say. "No, my brother. You have already passed through fire and water to travel across the Big Water to arrive at this place! Uncle Sam said finally, still pointing down the logging path to a newly-built house. Now you are at last coming to a *place of abundance!*"

<hr />

Jacob beheld the house of many rooms. Over the years, Sam had been praying "forgive us our debts as we forgive our debtors." All summer long, before leaving *Das Alte Landt* for the New World, Sam Fisher's uncanceled debt crept in and out of Father Jacob's mind, threatening to undermine Sam's noble intentions around the house of many rooms.

Father Jacob knew quite well that Annie was not willing to give up her desire for revenge over Sam's "unpardonable debt." Toxic thoughts lingered in the young preacher's mind, taking their toll upon his entire being. The expression on his face as he walked from room to room gave Sam only a fleeting sense of vindication from the uncanceled debt.

<hr />

I stayed with Barney and the wagon and watched my father closely. He was clearly overwhelmed by all the "brand newness" of the house and the spaciousness of each room. Knowing my father, he was in awe over how much his wife was going to love their place of abundance. As Father paced happily from room to room, Uncle Sam ran out to pulled me from the wagon seat.

"Sammy the Younger, my beautiful little boy! Just look at you, so suddenly a handsome little man already!" Uncle Sam threw me in the air, *as best he could*, and plopped me onto the end gate beside himself.

Father Jacob drove Barney back to the barn. Me and Uncle Sam still dangled our feet from the end gate. Mother stayed at Uncle Sam's shelter waiting for Father. So me and Uncle Sam walked Barney back to his pen in the lean-to.

<hr />

Father and Mother walked down the path to the house of many rooms. Uncle Sam led me to a humongous tree with friendly limbs reaching out all over, like it wanted to embrace me. "My praying tree," said my Uncle Sam casually, "where I go to talk with the Master, a friend who sticks closer than a brother."

I had never heard somebody talk about the Master in that way. Under a tree? A praying tree, no less? It "weirded" me out. But I wasn't letting nothing weird get in the way of the love I felt for Uncle!

"Do you come here often?"

⊷══⊙ ⊙══⊶

Annie bounced from room to room in the house that Sam built, chiding her man for accepting the house in the first place, like she was jealous or something. "He's just trying to make up for what he did to you!"

"I'd like to think it's because he loves me and has more opportunity than I have."

"Opportunity? Locked up in some penitentiary? Opportunity?"What's your brother trying to prove? What's he trying to take from you now?"

"He's not trying to take *anything*. He just wants to make things right. This house is his *peace offering.*"

"Peace offering! Well I guess! The man is *after* something. Can't you *see* that? What more could the man take from you than what he already has? You can't trust him; I tell you! Not even long enough to find out!"

"I have made a choice to forgive Sam. We must move ahead."

"Forgive him for what ? Listen to me Jacob. He stole your *Blessing, your very own blessing handed down from your forefather,* that's what! What he did is an abomination, a blasphemy against the Holy Ghost! It ain't forgivable. Your brother <u>owes</u> you! Can't you see that? He can beg for you to forgive him all you want. It's not going to do any good. Let *God* give back what your brother owes you! A <u>house</u> is never going to do it!"

Mother was not going to let anyone forget.

⊷══⊙ ⊙══⊶

Words of forgiveness had often formed secretly on their lips, but never this! *"Will you ever forgive me for what took place between us back there? We were only kids. We didn't realize what we were getting ourselves into. What I did was bad. I know I hurt you, my brother. It's always with me and weighs heavily on my spirit. Please forgive me. Will you? Can you?"*

Jacob was not prepared for such a direct question. "Who do I think I am *not* to forgive you? On the other hand, Samuel, for what you did, only God can forgive you. I will forgive as much as I am able to." That's all Jacob could manage.

"I have already asked God to forgive me, Jacob."

"And has He?"

"I believe He has."

"I am not the one who can forgive you, Sam. Only the Master can do that!"

"The nerve of that man! Asking forgiveness right off the bat! So boldly, and right in front of others, as if it was nothing! But that's just the way your brother is, always putting himself in front of you. Like he can only think of himself. What he did back there can never be *un*-done. Does he think forgiving him, just like that, will make the unforgivable go away?"

Annie wasn't even going to let *God* determine Sam's fate.

⊷⊷⊷ ⊶⊶⊶

Mother did not want to go to the New World and leave her beloved people behind. So she took it out on all of us – on Father one day and on me the next. Me and Father had this secret *pact* to stick together and not cave in. The more Mother ranted, the more eager Father Jacob and I were to get to the New World, and me to see my beloved Uncle Sam. Father never said much, which set Mother off all the more.

One day we settled into *the house of many rooms.* But then Mother nagged me and Father like never before. Mostly about all the attention we gave Uncle Sam, like she was always a little jealous of him. Mother made like she did not like what the house stood for in the first place. She nagged us about that too.

I was bewildered by our house of so many rooms. *"I wish I could be back to the Old Country. Life back there was a lot more simple!"*

Father Jacob noticed that I was not myself lately, then decided I needed to keep busy, somewhere away from the house. So he gave me over to Uncle Sam to be his *knecht* (hired hand). I tingled inside my skin, like I did the very first day in the New World. *"Now I can grow up in the shadow of the one who is my idol! I will work myself to death to please him. I can't imagine heaven being any better than this! Do you think I live with Uncle Sam too?"*

"We'll see once," my father said, meaning it could go either way – one a joy, the other not.

⊷═◦ ◦═⊶

"Der Herr needs a heavy *schlegel* to split this coarse *bluck*," Sam joked to his 10-year-old *knecht* the first day they went out to split logs, pressing a finger into his temple and flexing his great muscles. The lad loved working for his uncle. At once the two bonded like brothers.

Meanwhile, Father Jacob had become preoccupied with life matters. Through the distraction he was fast becoming a virtual stranger to his own son. The preoccupation had already begun in the Old Country for Jacob, and now it had followed him to the New World.

The distraction was especially hard for Sammy II. They had been keeping their formative young son in darkness during his curious pre-teen years. Little wonder the lad grew up with such a penchant for mischief and was driven to such fantasy. No wonder he looked forward to getting out and working for his favorite uncle.

And now, with riding his uncle's constant up and downs, he lived in confusion all the more. *"But I do pretty good for a such a little kid, don't I?"*

⤜⇒ ⇐⤛

Uncle Sam showed me how to catch the trolley to Lancaster. I found new ways to work off my boundless energy and to direct my *gwunnernossing*. The city had a pawnshop, where I'd go and look at stuff that was supposed to be hands-off. There I fondled the guns and handled the treasures, dreaming they were mine to handle and use. Maybe even to keep?

Little Big Heart had tattled about Uncle Sam going to the city to see a "head doctor." I strayed up and down the streets searching for signs of a head doctor and found nothing. Back home I was so mad and frustrated I felt like taking it out on any creature I could find. So I chased the mice from beneath the brush piles around the edge of the clearing, beating them with a stick and killing every last one I could find!

⤜⇒ ⇐⤛

From the time I was a toddler back in *Das Alte Landt,* I was used to having Uncle Sam around and seeing wonderful it was. Trotting away at his heels kept me happy and fulfilled. Whenever he was around, I smiled and laughed easily, specially when he jostled me and tousled my forever strubbly bangs. I never grew out of loving Uncle Sam like I did when I was a playful child. It's what made our move to the New World a thing of such enormous anticipation.

But that was then. As I watch Uncle Sam and his buddy Big Heart clear trees for lumber, I sense him becoming more and more distant. I never knew him to be distant like that. I didn't know how to act when I first noticed him start to turn so deeply serious.

Meanwhile, my nephew Sammy II, had grown up a lot during the time when he was a kid. He had changed a lot as well. The young gwunnernoss was drawn like a siren to his uncle Sam's "different-ness." He was disturbed by the sudden mood swings and could not figure out the awful downers. *"I wonder where he goes or what he does when he has these scary downers!*

The undying loyalty I had for my cherished uncle would eventually turn into a compelling need to see inside the dark person Uncle had become. I guess I was somehow expected to ignore it! However, I have to keep trying to hang in and deal with Uncle's downers as best I can. Still I often catch myself romanticizing about the good old days back when I was but a tyke and my uncle doted on me!

"One day my gwunnernoss will strike out in search of my own answers."

⊶⊜ ⊜⊷

Big Heart's young son was a wannabe warrior. A long time before, he had been a self-designated watchman over the white man's place in the woods. He did not know what to make of the drably-clothed white people who appeared beside the Pequea and invaded his charge. By their plain dress and non-threatening demeanor, the "intruders" did not appear to be all that hostile. However, the wannabe warrior stayed close to his lookout, curiously observing the white man's every move.

The young warrior felt a constant rush from watching Sammy II. Here was a boy his own age, perhaps a fellow warrior, perhaps a wannabe like him. Visions danced in the Indian boy's head of all he and the white boy would some day do together!

As the white man and the boy worked on the clearing, the native boy sat in the crotch of the big tree and watched. He did not feel hostile. He only wished that he could come down and help the young Amish boy with the pale white skin and the long yellow bangs in his eyes, just to be in his presence.

On days when the red-bearded white man had gone off to the village, the native boy managed to sit lower into the big tree, just out of sight. He watched the white boy at work, in slow and deliberate moves, wishing he would notice him and make the first move. Both were shy and pretended not to notice anyone was around.

Little Big Heart father, Big Heart, is best described as an *animal in* Native American circles, while his son is described as an *eagle* - solitary like an eagle, beady eyes. Most of all, he is majestic in youth holds his head high and whistles (especially when he swings from the vines).

Not long after Father Jacob arrived in the New World, Pequea Sam began feeling a certain void. He had not gotten the response he craved from his brother and certainly not from wife Annie. He retreated to his tree, nestled into the trunk, and looked up through the branches for an answer. *"Is that all there is to reconciling, after all this time of being absent from each other? Nothing but this hollowness?"*

Uncle Sam had not spoken all morning – not even a word. I felt abandoned. As he and I worked behind the shed, working the crosscut, my uncle looked weary. His eyes watered and he seemed far away. "Clear up the *hecka*," he ordered half-heartedly.

He walked into the woods, leaving me to work all by myself. *"I will clean up the hecka. For my Uncle Sam, anything!"*

As I diligently carried armload after armload of the sticks to the edge of the clearing to dry for the big bonfire, the native boy mustered the courage to come all the way out of the tree. "We go play?" He had been reading my mind!

The Native boy sported two large turkey feathers in a band around his head. "Father says that feathers are the symbols of majesty and freedom that embody the spirit of our brothers in the West," the boy expounded as best he could in broken English. He pulled one his feathers from his band and stuck it through the straw on my hat brim. Curious as usual, but now wary, I was totally taken in by the Native boy who outsmarted me by a mile!

He ran to the creek and I followed close behind, taken aback by the boy's quiet assertiveness. He showed me how to look for arrowheads buried in the bank of the creek where his people had done battle in the past.

Arrowheads

We whiled away the morning along the Pequea scouting for more of the beautiful arrowheads. I treasured every one I dug from the creek bank, especially the one that appeared to be covered with mud. I handed the mud-covered flint to my friend, watching him spit on the flint and rubbing it vigorously. I watched in amazement as the muddy arrowhead turned clean and white as snow right before my eyes!

"Look what I just found, a giant one!" I exclaimed sometime later when I came upon an oversized object, buried deep in the bank. It was obviously not an arrowhead.

"That was once an axe, used as a weapon and for digging!"

I watched closely as the Indian boy showed me how to fasten an arrowhead to the end of a long stick, turn it into a spear, and spear a target with his bow and arrow. In addition he now showed me how to wind a leather string around the large one to make it into axe for fighting or for digging. I envied the boy's skill and did what I could to copy what he did. *Some day I will be just as skilled as my Native friend!*

I treasured every one of the arrowheads and carried the best-looking ones in my pockets. All day I jingled them, like newly-found coins. *"These I will keep safe in my room upstairs in Father Jacob's new house!"*

Alas, Father Jacob came upon the skillfully-honed arrowheads in his son's room. He tickled the sharp tips and rolled them around in his hand. "I'll make good use of these babies!"

Father Jacob daydreamed and caught himself imagining what he had to do merit ownership as he continued daydreaming of battles along this or that creek bed. He day-dreamed of full-blown skirmishes, with shiny white flints flying everywhere through the air! Some stuck into live targets, and others found their way into creek beds to be spotted and then dug out by the likes of young pioneers like Sammy II and his Indian buddy!

The best of the arrowheads Father Jacob put into his pocket to be joined with his hunting knife and other small fix-it tools he carried with him just in case. Time and again he reached into his pocket to fondle the arrowhead and to tickle the sharp edges of the white flint. Out of habit, he began by tickling the edges of the perfectly shaped arrowhead and then marking subtle little designs on his arms and hands with the sharp white flint.

One day Mother came upon the rest of my arrowheads and took them from me. "Ay, first you pal around with that red-faced little savage. And now I find you with his 'weapons of warfare'!" she barked, beside herself with anger. "From this day on, you will no longer play with the hideous little heathen! And you can no longer live at your Uncle Sam's place!"

I threw myself at Uncle Sam's legs and held onto his knees. "I won't let go until you say that I can come back and live with you! I won't let go until you "bless" me, Uncle!"

"Does my nephew know what he asks? How can I ever again give <u>any</u> kind of blessing to <u>anybody</u>! How can I give the lad, much as I love

him, what was not mine to give in the first place? Another blessing! Really now?"

✦✦✦

The jealous mother isolated her son to his own house and confined him to his room to separate him from the Indian boy. She would release him back to the uncle only after he promised never to let her boy play with the Indian.

The adventure of collecting arrowheads in areas of bygone skirmishes led to other adventures in using the arrowheads in play battle. "My buddy Little Big Heart, had given me a set of his turkey feathers to stick into the rim of my straw hat and turned me into a true warrior. In spite of my mother, he worked patiently at making me into a skilled shooter from his home-made bow, in the very same style as Little Big Heart himself!"

Everyday Little Big Heart and I were growing closer, calling each other "brother" until I felt like a part of Big Heart's family and a wannabe member of his tribe. Big Heart had long before hooked up with Uncle Sam and was the mainstay in building Uncle's empire along the Pequea. Little Big Heart joined his father after I came along, and the three of us worked together until the way opened for Little Big Heart to teach me more stuff about his culture and to become my loyal playmate.

One day me and Mother had it out. Again she spouted her disapproval over spending all that time with my Indian pal so much that she could see my personality change before her eyes!

"I am now a man, Mother."

"You are not a man; you are a peanut. A snake sliding through the grass. You are as foolish as a turkey," she chided, referring to the feathers in my hat brim and then boldly yanking them out.

✦✦✦

Now and then, Jacob Fisher watched the goings-on between his son Sammy II and his Native American buddy. "Come, we swing on the vines!" announced the warrior. I hesitated, somewhere between excitement and terror, surprised that I would even have the guts to attempt such a wild ride. Having decided, I would dare it. *Now would be the time!*

My heart pumped wildly. Immediately my tummy was filled with knots! Before I knew it, the whole world was spinning out of control. My fingers let loose of the vine! I went flying off into space. I guess I was flirting with a lot of danger. But how I loved it!

Jacob watched with great interest to how the two of them hit it off so well, like the tightest of brothers! "Oh, how I wish I could have hit it off with my brother like my son Sammy II does with his Indian pal Little Big Heart. Oh, how I wish I could go back to the past, if only for a brief moment, long enough to start my own boyhood again with my long-lost brother!" Jacob murmured. "Oh how I long to erase my hateful past!"

From the time Jacob had set foot in the New World, he grappled constantly with his past. He felt hopelessly stuck, unable to move out of the ingrained hate he had already learned as a child. To boot, Jacob grappled constantly with the dogged self-righteousness he had learned from his father.

With each bout of grappling with his past, Jacob was developing a curious but dogged habit of digging into his pocket after his favorite arrowhead. He had become attached to the flint from the day he first began fondling the perfectly sharpened edges in Sammy II's upstairs bedroom in the house of many rooms that his Uncle Sam had built for Jacob and Annie's family. With arrow in hand, Jacob soon became an ace at "drawing" with it. In a matter of seconds the perfectly-shaped arrow in the deft fingers of its "artist" was able to "create" every which design – subtle, half-hidden designs on his arm or hand. Any sort of design, suited to that particular mood or moment.

Tattooing

Father Jacob appeared destined to self-destruction in one form or another by his hatred and unforgiveness. He inadvertently began this self-destruction when he innocently collecting arrowheads with his son Sammy II and his Indian buddy Little Big Heart. No one would ever have guessed, much less Father Jacob himself, that he would someday end up collecting and admiring his own son's arrowheads, just to mutilate himself! Seemingly aware of what he was doing, he got a rush out of carving an occasional "tattoo" here or there upon his own body, deliberately defiling "The Temple of the Holy Ghost!"

Chapter 10

Prosperity Amid Strife

The barns in Penn's Woods started out as lean-tos. Most of the farmers elaborated on their lean-to's by adding to them as needed in order to keep hay dry in summer and guard the animals from the hard winter during the early season in the New World.

Pequea Sam set the pace for the barns in the Colony. His barn started out like the others, first as a lean-to, then as a shed to store his land-clearing tools and house and his driving horse. He added a section on for him to sleep. His lean-to, combined with its own sleeping quarters and a shed was far more elaborate than all the others in his area of the Pequea. Early on, Sam Fisher was known as the "Pequea's pacesetter."

After Uncle Sam had cleared enough land on the outskirts of his project for his lean-to plus another building, he laid out the footprint for his barn. He assembled the skeleton on the ground for all four sides to the barn. Once the sides were formed, he called together a "frolic" to raise the skeleton of the barn and to attach each side to the foundation.

The English community watched with curious interest while the enterprising young Sam Fisher assembled the skeleton of the barn on the ground. "What's the young Amish whippersnapper up to now?" they asked one another over back fences. The youthful

Sam Fisher, intent to follow his agenda, continued to piece together the sections despite the curious English bystander.

Now and then a fellow church member took time away from his own pursuits to pitch in and help Sam with his ambitious project. Others came out of curiosity, piecing together in their minds what was going on. Still others came just to dispel some wild rumor.

On occasion an English neighbor joined in the hype, intending that by throwing in a bit of time and muscle alongside the energetic pacesetter, the neighbor could generate enthusiasm back at his own camp, at least enough to lend credence to his own project.

The entire Colony watched in quiet amazement at the energy the young pacesetter generated. However, Sam Fisher had a vision to follow. The smell of progress was in the air.

⊷═⊙ ⊙═⊶

Sam Fisher's success was celebrated on all sides of the church and the community, both for his abundant energy and his ability to make friends so readily. Making new acquaintances had become for him an easy matter, from resolving to make "a new friend every other day" while he was in the Catacombs. Back in the Old Country, Sam had chosen his friends wisely and borrowed much of his strength from them.

Pequea Sam savored the favor of church and community. He had a passion for enterprise and thrived on the high esteem his enterprising spirit brought him, like some idolatry. Sometimes he had the feeling he was some sort of tragic hero possessed by a tragic flaw, that his events were pre-determined by Fates setting the stage, leaving little to choice.

⊷═⊙ ⊙═⊶

There were those who for some reason or other could not acknowledge the worth that Pequea Sam was bringing to the Pequea community. With them Sam held little esteem after they thought they could not support his entrepreneurial momentum. One of them was Joe Feree, self-proclaimed civic leader and Town Father. One day Joe came upon Sam piecing together the skeleton for his hoped-for barn.

"Do you have plans to carry out all this?" Joe asked, motioning to the timbers in their places about the ground.

"Plans? Of course I have plans! Would I do all this if I did not plan to do it?" Sam continued, sweeping an impatient hand across the project in a way that belittled the Town Father.

"I mean "paper" plans, something for the town fathers to give you some guidance, some kind of direction!"

"I already got paper plans! Got 'em right here in my head! And I already *know* what direction I'm taking. I don't need your so-called paper plans. In my mind's eye I can already *see* the finished barn. So what need have I for *anybody* to give me *any* kind of direction?"

Now Joe Feree was miffed! He suddenly didn't give a hoot about the good relationship he had with Pequea Sam. Before the self-proclaimed town father drove away, he ordered Sam Fisher to cease everything until the town council *approved* and then *signed* the plans drawn up on paper. Uncle Sam threw up his hands and slammed his tools into the shed and stomped into the woods.

"I felt just horrible! After all the felling and sawing and splitting we had done for the lumber mill, I could no longer see a finished barn in my mind's eye. But Uncle Sam sure could. At one time I was plenty excited for him and very much caught up in the spirit of his barn project."

Uncle Sam's mind works as efficiently as a fine clock, and he lets nothing interfere with the clockwork. But now, with plans already locked in place, I'm surprised he gave in to Mr. Feree so easily, like it had been just some ordinary misunderstanding. I've seen how angry it makes my uncle whenever things don't move ahead like he wants them to.

"Knowing Uncle Sam, it ain't over yet! He'll just go somewhere and cool off, and then go right back to the ways things were in the first place. My uncle can handle the likes of a Joe Feree!"

→━○ ○━←

Word soon got around how that Joe Feree and his town cronies had stopped Uncle Sam dead in his tracks. However, a few of Uncle's friends came out of the woodwork to say how they supported him. Everyone decided his project deserved to keep moving ahead.

One day a big part of the community – church, neighbors, and the like, came marching down the lane. Each one was carrying their own sets of tools, and dug in to Sam's project. Uncle scurried here and there on the skeleton and busily supervised the already-formed sections of the framework. Like a skilled craftsman with his head in place, he supervised the neighborhood muscle power, turning the surprise event into a celebrated happening. They called it a "barn raising."

At the end of the day, all four sides of our new barn stood proudly out of the ground. All sorts of friends and neighbors scrambled over the roof and along the sides, like a colony of ants.

Like a giant mushroom, our new barn had sprouted up out of the ground. All this in one single day! Not one in all of Penn's Woods – church people, English neighbors, not even Billy Penn himself – had ever witnessed such clockwork as went off at the hands of my Uncle Pequea Sam!

Now the tongues wagged like "all sam hill," like it was "just too much" for anybody the likes of this lowly young Amish whippersnapper to pull off such an undertaking. In a single day four sides of the largest barn in all of the Colony -- all the way to the roof -- stood at the spot where the day before there had been only an open space. It seemed like even the church people were proud to be part of such an ambitious undertaking, seeing as they came by all the more to chip in their muscle power.

Tongues wagged among the town fathers as well. Angry tongues and wounded egos came out of the woods to serve the Green-eyed Monster Envy. Now Pequea Sam with his "idolatry" was in trouble for sure!

⋅→⟹ ⟸←⋅

The Town Council members were up in arms about the way that Uncle Sam went ahead with his project in the manner that he did, and stirring up such a ruckus. They couldn't decide whether the young Amishman was the one stirring up the ruckus in the first place, or whether the church and the church neighborhood were just feeling sorry for Pequea Sam.

Everybody was of the opinion that Uncle Sam had put far too much effort in his barn project only to be denied permission to go forward with things. A number of the people decided that certain members of the self-appointed town council were downright bullying Sam. Everybody was mad about that too.

Several of the so-called town fathers later decided that those same members were overstepping their bounds and were getting much too "power hungry" and decided it was necessary just to over-ride the "thrown-together" town council. When several of the council members said they were going to "back down" they did it to suggest that the council may have indeed been taking advantage of Uncle Sam. The council members rapidly took sides on the issues.

With that, the town citizens also took sides, as well as several of the more out-spoken church members.

Finally the entire church district got caught up in the ruckus.

⊷═◌ ◌═⊷

The barn raising was over and done. The town fathers, Joe Feree for one, were miffed that they had not been able to stop Uncle Sam – well-intentioned to some, an arrogant whippersnapper to others – from moving forward back there while he was hustling around putting the skeleton together on the ground. The council had not taken the bull by the horns on time, so that they lost their "strong position" and had to find some way to stop the forward progress in midstream.

Although our new barn was already standing and under roof, there was still a whole lot left to complete the barn. So Joe Feree did my Uncle Sam dirty by issuing a *Cease-and-Desist Order,* mandating that nothing more could be done until Uncle had a "Binding Agreement" to move ahead without further permission. Meaning that if Uncle Sam took one more step forward on his own, he would be "held in contempt." He would have to tear down the whole barn, which they now had declared "an unlawful structure."

Joe Feree's Order was delivered to the job site and nailed on all four sides of our new barn while a handful of neighbors and friends were working. The nailing of the summons created a disturbance up and down the Pequea and became fodder for earnest tongue-wagging at every village corner. The town fathers bragged about the distraction they had created and about all the opinions they caused to be bandied about.

Uncle Sam had always been extra careful not to make waves among his church people and among his community of *well-wishers.* Now suddenly he began "feeling" the stares and receiving the brunt of the *tongue-waggers.* Seemed that Uncle was being persecuted because of bad blood coming from those who envied him for his success.

⊷═▷ ◁═⊶

One day Uncle Sam musta had enough. Driven to the breaking point by the very people he loved and served, he walked away from our half-built barn. *Talk about hurting!*

I hurt all the way into my core when Joe Feree handed my beloved uncle the *Cease-and-Desist Order,* right before the eyes of those he loved and respected. As usual, uncle traipsed off to be by himself and the chance to think things over, this time sober-faced and resigned.

Me and Little Big Heart watched him walk to his usual place in the woods. He parked at the foot of what he called his *Meditation Tree.* Me and Little Big Heart called the special tree "Uncle Sam's Hangin' Tree" because of the many limbs stretching out all over the place. Uncle Sam wrestled with his entire being underneath the giant Sycamore, until he fell asleep.

Me and my Native American pal climbed up into the big Sycamore and waited for Uncle Sam to wake up. We stared quietly into the sky with really no thoughts except for the hope that we would discover an answer for Uncle problems somewhere in the friendly clouds.

I told Little Big Heart about a story I had picked up a long time ago. A very short man named Zacchaeus climbed into a big Sycamore tree so that the Master could spot him in up in the tree as He was passing by below and throw the short man His blessing. The Master did indeed notice the little man up in tree. Not only did He notice the little man, but his Master ordered him to come down from the Sycamore and receive his blessing!

"Will the Master notice me and Little Big Heart, like He did the little man Zacchaeus, up here in the middle of Uncle's Prayin' Tree?"

⊶⇒ ⇐⊷

The following day, late in the afternoon, Uncle Sam and I went back to his project. We picked up all the remnants of lumber not nailed in place and stacked them into neat little piles. Uncle Sam looked so sad, and I was afraid he might crumble into one of his heaps again.

Uncle did not talk much after that, although it was clear that he was deeply grateful for the humongous way friends and neighbors had contributed to the community. Getting folks together to work on his building projects had raised the spirit of the people and encouraged friendship among all kinds of people. Only thing now, nothing could assure my uncle that the barn raising had been the right thing after all!

⊶⇒ ⇐⊷

I got to thinking how I was learning all this private stuff about my uncle I had no business knowing about. I was feeling mighty guilty, and the guilt followed me everywhere. Now I felt especially guilty about going to see the painted lady at her house in the city.

I wanted desperately to walk inside my uncle's skin to see what he was up to when he went away like this. *"But I can't, which should mean it's none of my business* what *Uncle does!* I decided once and for all mind my own business, flinging dirt clods at a turkey buzzard perched on a nearby stump mocking me.

I felt guilty not telling Father Jacob about the house with a red light I saw Uncle Sam go into. Maybe Father Jacob could help Uncle see what a big mistake he's making. *"Surely it wouldn't be safe telling Father anything like that, being the preacher and all. Then Mother not liking Uncle in the first place. Anyhow not in our neighborhood with all those wagging tongues!"*

Rumors flew throughout the district like a house afire, flaming down the line after one well-meaning wag tells another, each remembering half of what they heard and making up as much, ever adding fuel to the flames. *"I don't gotta tell anybody anything, specially when it's not the affair of us little ones. Father Jacob, simple as a dove and sly as a fox, has his own ways of finding out stuff when he wants to!"*

"It's not what they say about me that hurts; it's what they *whisper*," my uncle said on a contemplative day. Seems he wanted to feed me information too adult and too confusing for my young mind. Maybe he thought I'd been hearing things about him and was trying to cover something over, maybe uncover something.

"I call them whisperers because they talk behind your back and not to your face. The stuff they whisper about goes up and down the neighborhood; and every time it does, somebody adds more or changes something they already heard. Sometimes it comes out the other end way different from the way it went in. The whisperers are the same ones who'll smile at you and make like everything's hunky-dory, when all the time they're talking trash behind your back!

Things began getting all confusing to me. I love my uncle and it hurts when they say stuff behind his back. I want to believe he would not be somebody that anybody would whisper about. But they do it, because now and then I hear their kids do it as well!

Sometimes it got confusing for Uncle Sam too, I'm sure. Here was a smart man, who knows a bad spirit when he's around one, yet he chooses to turn and look the other way and not think bad about the whisperers. Uncle takes a bad person as he finds him and tries not to see any bad in him.

Uncle Sam is so much bigger than those who go around putting him down, and that's why he's so far above the rest. Uncle Sam is a great man in my eyes, and nobody has any business talking trash about him. It's easy to see that what the whisperers do just makes everything bad.

⊷═◉ ◉═⊷

Knowing all this "back-around" stuff about Uncle Sam sometimes created a distance between us and felt like a separation. *"What ever happened to the Uncle Sam I used to cherish so much back in the good old days? The one who loved me like the son he didn't have, who said I was the apple of his eye and tickled my belly and tossed me in the air and tousled my bangs so that I like keeping them strubly?"*

It hurt like the mischief when Uncle Sam began later on to treat me like I was some kind of "grown-up" when I was not near done being a child. *"Did life in the penitentiary cause Uncle Sam to be the way he is now? Were there so many ups and downs in prison that he got used to living so unsteady that he needed the help of a head doctor? With the lady with the red light, of all people?"*

Or maybe my uncle starting to treat me "like some kind of grown-up" because I was just getting too nosy? Well maybe I just couldn't help that part of it, because I was not near done being a child?

⊷═◉ ◉═⊷

For Sam Fisher it was something far deeper than any prison that made his life unsteady. It was because he lived in the "prison of the mind." It was about a fractured relationship with his flesh and blood, made worse by his own emotional and chemical imbalance.

More than anything, Sam Fisher struggled constantly with the need to become worthy of his father's *Blessing*, which he had gotten by his stepmother's deceit. In order to prove himself worthy of the

Blessing, or to live above the deceit, young Samuel thought he had to be successful and prosperous, to be "top dog!"

He had left the Old Country in order to find himself and to earn the fear and respect he so desperately craved. Alas, the hunger for fear and respect had subtly and slowly begun "seeping into the relationship" with Sammy II, his young *knecht*.

There were times when the uncle would forget that the youngster was but a boy and found it difficult to relate to him as such. The uncle craved his nephew's fear and respect so much that now and again he would end up *losing it* for trying so hard to *demand* it. Simply *feeling entitled* to his nephew's fear and respect, was taxing the relationship as well.

⊷⇒ ⇐⊷

Uncle Sam came back from the village in a bad fix. "How'd the meeting go, Uncle?" I asked helpfully.

"I'll nail his hide to the barndoor," he mumbled.

Uncle, even in a good mood, was not one to talk about what he had just been going down with him. I was too young to know what went on inside his skin anyhow, so all I could was ride the ups and downs with him. Today I got to ride another downer!

Uncle had gone to the bank to get money for a set of buildings on the spot which we had been clearing off. Joe Feree voted against helping Uncle get the money to finish the barn. "Let the man finish what he already got going!" said Joe Feree right off, the bite of envy casting his vote.

I was wishing I could ask Uncle to tell me what happened in town that made him come home so angry, but was afraid he would bite my head off if I asked him one more thing. I unhitched Barney as my out-of-fix uncle walked away without bothering to help. *"Yuk, smells like medicine of the worst kind!"*

He had left me to take care of Barney. I went into the feed entry to throw Barney a scoop of oats and found my uncle on the hay pile with his arms across his eyes. I watched his chest rise and fall, then tippy-toed back out of the feed entry. *"Methinks he got hit on the bluck with a mighty heavy schlegel! I just hope he feels better once he wakes up. By then maybe he'll forget all about nailing anybody's hide to anybody's barndoor!"*

⊹⊳═○ ○═⊲⊹

Sometime later Uncle Sam sent word for me to come to the village to pick him up. I hung the reins over the lantern at the trolley stop and hurried into the waiting area, so proud of my duty! We walked out together and climbed into the hackaround. *"Was it good trip?"*

My uncle usually fussed and made me feel recognized and wanted. But so far he had said nothing. I knew not to ask about his trip again, or talk about anything for that matter, when he was like this. It was a clear sign that something was wrong when I had to come fetch him to begin with. My uncle usually walked back from the village.

Uncle Sam climbed up over the wheel and sat down heavily. "I can't live like this anymore," he mumbled. "One way at home and another way out here in town!"

"Huh?" I tried to sound interested in what he meant.

"Gae," he ordered sharply, pointing with his chin. Uncle kept his eyes down and his head still and said nothing all the way home. Something must have gone really wrong!

⊹⊳═○ ○═⊲⊹

Uncle Sam had gone to the village to take care of business. The day had started out as just another downer for him. He left me with orders to turn a section of sod and to break up the lumps and prepare another section ready for planting.

Around the middle of the afternoon I went into the woods looking for my uncle, thinking that maybe he had stopped there after returning from the village. He was not at his tree, and I could not leave my curiosity alone. My gut told me to run back out to the village and look for Barney and the hackaround *"Maybe I can find out where the head doctor lived. It won't hurt nothing."*

Barney stood faithfully at the hitching post outside the government building. Uncle Sam was likely in Joe Feree's office. Careful not to draw attention to myself, I walked right by good old Barney and ignored him. But as I walked by, he schnobbled loudly. I walked even faster for fear I was drawing attention to myself by being where I had no business being. I turned around and hurried back home, where I belonged in the first place.

It was a hot day. The late-afternoon breeze cooled the sweat running down my back and into my broadfalls. What I had discovered in the village made my head spin. Raucous laughter poured from inside the *Vatshous* (saloon), all the way into the street to where I had stood watching. I could hear uncle above everybody. It pained my spirit oh so deeply to discover that my uncle was mingling with the English folk inside the village *Vatshous*, the worst kind of roadhouse, no less!

Uncle Sam had been so stern and quiet lately that the vision of what must have been going on inside that door, stuck in my mind long after I got back to the field. But I trusted my uncle to be conducting business, like he said he was gonna do, and not be hanging out at a *Vatshous*, of all places! Especially after the way he spoke of living "one way at home and another way in town." Or about the many temptations of those "living close to any kind of roadhouse."

"But then how shall I explain away my Uncle sleeping in the feed entry with his arm across his face?"

⌐══ ══⌐

I turned into a little gwunnernoss one more time after Uncle Sam kept disappearing so much of the time. One day I couldn't contain myself and went out to look for him, starting with the area someplace around his favorite *"Prayin' Tree."* Sure enough, all morning Uncle had been sitting underneath his tree, looking for refuge under its mighty wings.

He'd been there so often lately that the grass under the tree was shaped like his bottom where he had leaned back against its mighty trunk. I turned in my tracks after my curiosity was satisfied and went back to sweeping out the shed, *for the third time.* My mind was filled with the concerns I had been feeling lately for my beloved Uncle Sam!

⌐══ ══⌐

Sam and Barney came down the lane and cut into the field where I had been stomping out clods. *"Wie machsht aus?"* he asked. In one long motion he threw the lines over the brake lever, vaulted out over the wobbly yellow wheel on the hackaround, lifted my tattered straw hat, and tousled my sweaty bangs. I sure needed the validation!

"Goot, Uncle," I said sheepishly, suddenly feeling enormously good.

"Gwunnernoss dehet der Kotz!" my uncle said, half in jest but looking deeply into my eyes. I had heard the expression before -- about curiousity killing the cat. I wondered why my uncle would say that to me now, and so emphatically. Enough for me to suspect he knew something.

- 147 -

He must have sensed I'd been up to the village!

⊷⟹ ⟸⊶

Now and then Uncle Sam wanted to be let alone, and didn't like me chattering away at him during those times. He knew where to go to be by himself. Some of those times I was beside myself to know where he had been.

"*When you go way, Uncle, where do you usually go?*"

"I go to a therapist that's where, if you have to know. I go to have sessions and to see my *head doctor*. He helps me to figure out why some days are dark and the sun don't shine." However, the so-called sessions with Uncle Sam and his *head doctor* were beginning to last longer and longer.

"*I can't help it, but I gotta start spying again! Just a wee bit, only one time!*"

⊷⟹ ⟸⊶

They sat behind Joe Feree's house, holding brown bottles in their calloused fingers and getting louder by the minute. Uncle Sam had lied to me! I had looked everywhere in the village for a head doctor and there was none. I was disappointed and angry that my Uncle Sam would even say there was a therapist in the village in the first place, let alone that he had gone to have his so-called sessions with him. I think something's been going on!

"*No wonder Uncle Sam he wants me to mind my own business and not ask him one more question!*"

On the other hand, nobody questioned *anything* "Sam Fisher" did, so what right did I have in doing it? And so I let it go – had to – because if I told him he fooled me, that there was no such head doctor in the whole village, he'd tell me to mind my own business

148

for sure, and then some! He'd probably say that I was the fool for being so nosy to begin with.

Uncle was right. It was my gwunnernoss that always got me into trouble. So I swallowed the hurt and went about my business being the *knecht*. *"Tough to heeltrot anyhow, when my hero doesn't want me coming up behind him!"*

＊⇒ ⇐＊

"Sammy II, suppose you hitch Barney to the hackaround and drive me to the trolley – you and the Indian boy," my uncle ordered lovingly. Little Big Heart did it for my uncle lovingly. *After all, what else was left for us to do?*

Coming back from the trolley station, me and Little Big Heart were sad beyond words, hopeless to know why Uncle Sam was going to see a head doctor yet again. This time about something he brought on by his own doing and then could not control!

On the way back from dropping my Uncle off, Little Big Heart dropped a bombshell that explained everything. "Did you know your uncle Sam goes to see this lady in the city what smokes cigarettes and what paints her lips!" my Indian brother blurted out of the blue.

Little Big Heart's sudden bombshell stuck right in my gizzard, and it really hurt. For a long I was silent, angry but silent. *"What's it of the little Indian's business <u>what</u> my Uncle does when he goes off to the city like this afternoon? And what's it of his business <u>who</u> my Uncle keeps company with? And what business is it of his if she <u>does</u> smoke cigarettes and paints her whole face if she wants to?"*

The little Indian saw how mad I was. Little Big Heart stayed quiet as a mouse the whole way back from delivering my Uncle to the trolley station. His father Grosse Hertz, had taught the little Indian that way. How to stay quiet, and in true Native American fashion not to make any more waves after he saw how mad I was!

Barney was always glad whenever Little Big Heart and me could drive Uncle Sam anywhere. We always fussed and cackled like hens when we were alone after dropping his uncle off anywhere. But not tonight!

Barney musta noticed how quiet Little Big Heart and his master were, all the way back with from the trolley station. *"My favorite pal is gonna be sad all the way home 'cuz he saw how mad I was and not saying one measly word! So will I!"*

We stayed quiet the whole time we were unhitching Barney, never saying a measly word! Still not saying one measly word the whole time when we were throwing Barney his portion of oats!

⋅►═◐ ◑═◄⋅

Earlier on, Uncle Sam had shown me how to catch the trolley to the city. I knelt on the seat so I could reach the string so a bell would ring next to the trolley master's head to tell him when we wanted off. I remembered how Sam smiled and talked to the master. I was all puffed up and *grossfeelich,* riding the trolley with Uncle, the magic of wheels hugging the tracks and the huge car tickling my hiney as it moved into place under me.

Today I would be doing the magic all by myself!

⋅►═◐ ◑═◄⋅

On another day, I was going back to the big city to see whether Uncle had been there, but I was angry because I had not gotten anywhere. Back home, I pretended to *shoot rats* running in and out of my uncle's brush piles at the edge of the clearing. All afternoon I was bored and rooted mice from the edge of Barney's haystack and beat them with a big, long stick as my weapon, killing everything I saw.

At first I was more than a little angry when Little Big Heart dropped the bombshell about Uncle Sam going to see a madam in the city. *"Today I will go to the big city to 'investigate' the lady what smokes cigarettes and what paints her lips. I hafta see for myself what the little Indian gwonnernoss was so busy fussing about!"*

I strayed up one street and down the other to where I thought her fancy house would be, hoping for another glimpse at the good-smelling English lady and longing for more of the affection she gave me the day she found me standing by her gate asking about Uncle.

I waited just outside the gate to the English lady's place. For a long time I stood and looked through the ornamental bars. After a while a paint-up lady opened the door with the red lamp and acted like she had known me for a long time. She flicked her cigarette into the rosebush and came out to the gate, grinning like she knew where the little black hat belonged.

"My uncle lied to me again!"

The English lady walked with me through the gate. Her arm was tight around my shoulders. She smelled oh so wonderful, like the fanciest of all perfumes, and all I did was cry. My cherished uncle was still keeping company with some painted-up English lady. That was suddenly too much for my young sensibilities, and all I knew was how to cry!

I told the lady just how I felt, sparing nothing. Suddenly I wasn't ashamed of *anything.* I told her how I'd been sneaking past her house, hoping that no one saw me sneaking around her place. And how that today I stood right at her gate and did not care if she *did* see me.

"Uncle Sam is my idol and I fear for him. I'm scared to death he'll get in all kinds of trouble with the church and the neighbors. If my uncle gets in trouble then I'm in trouble too. And now I'm going to be in all kinds of trouble for sure when he finds out I came here. But most of all, my uncle is in trouble with the Lord in Heaven!"

The lady looked at me long and hard, like she was looking right through me. "Look at me," she said. Her big green eyes and long lashes were so full of pity that I thought she was about to cry, too. She pulled me to her, where it was warm and soft, and then bussed my cheek.

"You better hurry on home now," she said, and then let me cry against her warm, sweet-smelling breast.

⊶═▷ ◁═⊷

It was clear that Uncle Sam was gone for the day. Me and my Indian pal traipsed around in the woods, killing time, always trying to spot one more flint. We came open uncle's *Hangin' Tree.* We read each others minds the minute we beheld the many inviting arms. *"Another woods game!"*

This time we chased each other with weapons until one overcame the other and indicated victory or defeat with a stabbing motion. We chased each other from limb to limb and from tree to tree, Little Big Heart in loincloth and me in my work duds. I got really good at evading the attack of the enemy who was "it" considering how my broadfalls created constant "wedgies" and slowed me down.

"Native boy wears only loincloth but more quicker than white boy wearing broadfalls!" We played our games with increasing fervor, communicating a fierceness with grunts and whoops. We communicated that part very well.

The object of "it" was for chasor to pursue chasee with his "weapon" – a long stick – that "poisoned" the one being pursued, in turn making him "it." The "it" word fascinated the native boy and he loved repeating it – each pointing to the other and tauntingly proclaiming him "it!"

In the clearing I would start out being "it" since that was my territory. In the woods, however Little Big Heart was "it" like he was chasing me out of his territory. The name we invented for our game was "it." For us "it" had a much deeper meaning. But we were never hostile about "it" as the grown-ups were who came before us.

We were the best of pals, the wannabe warrior and the boy with the strubled yellow bangs. The games continued as we fished the Pequea for sunnies and carp. Sometimes we even went for a casual swim in the muddy water. I was ashamed of my naked body and tried to hide my nakedness. Little Big Heart certainly didn't mind *any* nakedness, as we sat and babbled about everything yet nothing at all!

⊷━▷ ◁━⊷

Sammy II was distressed by how his beloved uncle was covering his besetting sins by pretending to be a model member of the church. *"There are no shortcuts to the promised land,"* his uncle used to say. The young lad had watched his uncle prosper and prayed it would continue despite the two faces he was wearing.

I was not sleeping well because I was worried continuously about Uncle Sam. One night I dreamed the very thing I feared most of all if my uncle kept on going to see the painted lady in her fancy house.

Uncle Sam was standing on the highest beam in the barn shouting directions to his carpenters. It was a windy day and there was no support to keep the beam from swaying back and forth. I clambered onto the beam and came up behind Uncle on my hands and knees, hugging the swaying beam for all I was worth. But Uncle Sam walked defiantly along the length of the beam as if there was he saw no danger.

"Stop, Uncle! Please stop. You MUST stop, Uncle!" I called out with all my might. Uncle looked back and turned away quickly, ignoring me as he kept on walking toward the end of the beam. He looked into my eyes and disappeared over the edge. Pain stabbed into the very core of my soul, and I woke up crying "Uncle! Uncle!

But no one was there to hear me crying uncle!

⊷═▷ ◁═⊷

This morning Uncle Sam came in from the woods and was in a really good mood, better than he had been in a while. "Let's work the acres, my son, and prepare them for maize," he said. "The seed catches on so much better when the ground has been prepared." Preparing the ground meant pulling out stumps and picking up rocks. Work was easier and time moved faster whenever Uncle was his good old self, and today felt like it would be a wonderful one.

Mid-forenoon Uncle announced he must go to the village and see his therapist – "head doctor" as he called him – and suddenly it was not such a wonderful day after all. My heart had broken in pieces after my uncle lied to me about a head doctor in the village and I found there was none anywhere in the village. Now my heart broke all over again. Uncle Sam had lied to me again, and did not believe he was going to the village at all.

The two-acre field began to look humougous now that I had to tackle the ground-preparing all by myself. If I was going to feel any better I would have to see for myself what Uncle Sam was up to. *"This will be the perfect time to sneak the trolley into the city!"*

As soon as I sat down on the trolley seat, I suddenly became paralyzed with fear. *"What would Uncle Sam say if he actually discovered me in the city? What would I ever say to him?"*

I walked up one street and down another, always keeping the trolley tracks in sight. I couldn't find my uncle anywhere, because I didn't know where to look for him in the first place.

My desire to *heeltrot* Uncle Sam had been driving me bananas lately, and now it was causing me to go spy on him. But the city was so much bigger now that I was lost in it and all by my lonesome.

So I gave up searching for Uncle and found a "trolley hut" where I waited for the next car to take me home.

⊷▬⊜ ⊜▬⊶

Uncle Sam had been acting strange the last several days – very much inside himself and never speaking – the same way he always did just before he went off to talk to his tree or sneak away to the city. This time he was gone for two days and I thought I was not going to find him. My curiosity got the best of me and I went on a journey.

I cut through the woods and across the fields and got to the trolley station before Uncle did, praying earnestly that the trolley master would not tell my uncle I had caught the trolley one run before.

I got off near the edge of the city and waited for the next trolley to pass. I ducked for cover behind a lilac tree when I saw a black hat in the front of the trolley. When I spied my uncle having the usual banter with the trolley master, I leaped from behind the bush and chased the car as fast as my legs would carry me to where Uncle Sam got off three stops later. I snuck in behind him and trailed him down a quiet side street. He hurried through a fancy ornamental gate and up to the porch. He looked cautiously around himself and hurried through a door with a red lamp burning on the right doorpost.

All the way home on the trolley, my mind began doing flip-flops and gave me no rest. All the next day I pouted. *"Sometimes I just feel like hiding somewhere and crying my eyes out!"*

"What bothers you, Son?"

"Nothing."

"Not so! Why all day you walked around with your head down. You never did that before. But you sure are doing it now! Look at me when I'm talking to you, Sammy II! Now tell me what's ailing you!" The way Uncle talked to me made me clam up all the more.

"It's about your head doctor!"

"My head doctor? What about my head doctor?"

"Why does he have a red light on his doorpost?"

I knew right away I'd said the wrong thing when I looked up. Uncle Sam had turned bull-angry. He never looked at me like he did just then. "I think you need to go back to the Old Country!"

I darted into the woods. I ran til I couldn't run anymore and went in and out of naps underneath a friendly tree. When I finally awoke, every tree looked the same. Suddenly I got so scared that I'd be forever lost! But I stuck out in what I hoped would be the right direction. I followed my nose and prayed until at last I spied the long limbs off in the distance!

"In Das Alte Landt, I was the shadow of my uncle Sam, but in the New World I am the cry of a lonely young wolf!"

⊷═▭ ▭═⊶

I was finding out the hard way that now and then Uncle flies off the handle because he doesn't like people butting into his business! Much less me! When Uncle he goes on me like he just did, I think it's because of me spying and I get scared that he's going to send me back to the Old Country.

It's all my fault when Uncle goes off on me. I must be more careful to mind my own business after all the fussing he's been doing about wanting to be let alone and not have other people tell him how he oughtta do stuff. *"Every day I'm afraid he's going to take it out on me and say he don't want me around anymore either and then send me back to live in Mother's house. Going back there would be about as bad as going back to the Old Country. I want to live in Uncle's hogan and not anywhere else!*

⊷═▭ ▭═⊶

Some days I feel like I don't belong to anybody anymore and I get really lonely. I'm scared to get too close to Uncle lately because he might bite my head off. *"It's a lonely time for a chatterbox like me when people just don't talk and I don't know what they're thinking!"*

There were times after that when Uncle seemed so inside himself in thought like he'd forget where he was or what he was just about to do. Sometimes he stayed all quiet and made like he was far away somewhere. It was like he was losing a piece of his life. The parts that used to be filled with adventure, success, power. It was as if those parts of my uncle were gone and might never come back and be part of him again.

From the time I remembered anything, I idolized Uncle Sam as the perfect hero. Since coming to the New World his image heightened all the more. I was convinced he was perfect and wished I could spend every waking moment somewhere close to him. *"But recently I am having disturbing second thoughts concerning rejection and my beloved uncle!"*

⋗═══ ═══⋖

The greatest terror that Sammy II could possibly have felt was that he was not loved, and rejection was the hell he feared. Once he began feeling rejected, he found rejection in places where it did not even exist. Worse yet, he drew forth rejection from people by flat-out "expecting" it!

⋗═══ ═══⋖

Over time I was discovering some of Uncle Sam's hidden faults from working around him and by spending time with him. His worst faults are those he managed to hide from his neighbors and especially from his own church people. *"I've heard is said that a self-righteous person does not recognize his own faults and neither do those who know him best and love him most."* That's how it is with me and Uncle Sam.

Sure, I have my hidden faults too. One fault I have is in carrying stuff inside my mind about Uncle Sam that I have no business knowing. It's like carrying around an extra load, to know all this stuff my uncle is hiding from people. *"Worst of all is the stuff he manages to keep hidden from Father Jacob, my own pop, and from his our own church people!"*

⊶⊷⊷ ⊶⊷⊷

I took Uncle's latest dressing down to mean that maybe I was okay with him again, that maybe I could even heeltrot again. *"If I know Uncle, he'll overlook my transgression of spying on him, but he's never going to forget!"*

Now and then I feared he would go off on me again, and a million rubber bands tightening around my head. Today it happened again.

"What're we doing today, Uncle?" I asked, fishing for an answer and trying to sound cheerful. He was deep in thought and grunted something, then turned his head to spit tobacco juice.

And now Uncle Sam was not talking to me except in short little grunts. Little did I realize that when he and I started coming apart was because was hurting deep inside his skin, just like I was.

The longer my uncle stayed silent like this, the harder he worked. *"Sometimes I'm scared that something really bad is gonna happen!"*

There were also times when Uncle seemed so inside himself that he'd forget where he was or what he was just about to do. Sometimes he stayed all quiet and made like he was far away somewhere. It was like I was losing a piece of his life, the parts that used to be filled with adventure, success, and power. *"Sometimes I am afraid these parts of my beloved uncle are gone and might never come back and be part of him again!"*

⤙═◯ ◯═⤚

Tonight Uncle Sam said nary a word when he got home. I felt like I was some kind of stranger in his house because he treated me like one. Perhaps that's what I "needed" for spying on him. But I was so attached to him that I thought that I could not let him out of my sight. The worst thing I could ever have done to wreck things between us was to spy on him. *"But I did, didn't I? Sometimes it's like I am driven to do it and couldn't help myself!"*

Just thinking about him all afternoon, my head was doing *flip-flops. "I wonder what Uncle Sam will do once he gets home? I worry that he has been changing into something different. But why am I only one noticing? What if he gets home some day and be so different that he won't care about me anymore?"*

I had learned from my Native American family how to crawl inside a cocoon and get away from stuff that bugged me and threatened to rip my world apart. Inside the cocoon I learned to shut out my feelings as though I did not have any.

"Little Big Heart and his family are going to be my new cocoon!"

⤙═◯ ◯═⤚

The Painted Lady spoke highly and with great respect to Sammy II regarding his uncle. It was obvious she had high regard for her client. "Your uncle has a personality that draws many friends onto himself. Wherever he is, when he's feeling good, his presence causes people's minds to be erected marvelously."

"Yup, my uncle is full of life and muscle. But he sure can go off when he ain't feeling so good. In a heartbeat he can go off when he's not feelin' good!"

- 159 -

The respect that the Painted Lady held for Pequea Sam rose even higher after she had become friends with his nephew Sammy II. So much so that caught herself fantasizing about him as a part of her new-found *freindschaft* like she once had his uncle.

At the same time the lad fantasized about the madam. *"What would it be like, having a painted mother, all decked out in fancy ornaments!"*

Pequea Sam entrusted the madam with anything that was on his heart. But he guarded fiercely anything having to do with his cherished nephew. Now it became clear to Sam that the madam had indeed become friends with Sammy II. Nevertheless, Sam would not let her so much as *hint* about any friendship his madam may have made with any flesh-and-blood relative for fear of losing his standing within his own *freindschaft*.

⤙══ ══⤚

It was dark when Uncle Sam walked down the lane, worn out and sweaty, and stretched out on the floor of the hogan. He was having another one of his "headaches" and I knew enough to leave him alone.

He had stopped at Joe Feree's house on the way back from the city to get to the bottom of things with Joe. They had gotten the bottom of things all right. All they got to the bottom of was one more bottle! Neither one had the wherewithal to finish the real business Uncle Sam had stopped to talk to Joe about. Anyway, he looked pretty comfortable sprawled on the hogan floor!

In the afternoon Uncle came upon me sitting under his *meditation tree.* His tree was off-limits to anybody else but him. I knew that, but I went there anyway because I thought it was a way to get next to him. He was not mad!

"You come along now, Sammy II; this is not the place for you," Uncle said, pulling at my shirt sleeve.

"Tell me Son, is there any reason why you need to tell your pop about the house with the red lamp?" His question caught me by surprise and stuck in my throat. Uncle knew I'd been to see the Painted Lady!

"*Why no!*" I blurted, sobbing before my uncle could finish his question. "*No! Not ever! I would never do such a thing!*"

"Look Son, I promise I won't go to the house with the red lamp ever again if you promise me not to follow me anymore. Not to the village, not to the trolley, not anywhere! You hear?"

"*I promise with all my heart that I will never to tell Pop!*" I said, still sobbing, feeling that Uncle had just taken me apart and was never going to put me back together again!

"*But I just kept on spying because Uncle was rejecting me so much! If only my uncle knew that! If only I could have told him so!*"

⊷▭◌ ◌▭⊶

After the confrontation with the town fathers and the day Joe Feree nailed that *Cease-and-Desist Order* on the side of our half-built barn, the barn stayed put. No more building; no more nothing! The message had been clear enough.

Uncle Sam had always been the smart one in this mess, and I was just waiting for him to find a way to see our half-built barn to its end. "The next one that makes a move, or even says the first word, loses," said Uncle. "We call it *giving away the store!*"

"*But we've already given up the store! We're already the losers, ain't we, Uncle? Look how everything has turned quiet ever since the day Mr. Feree nailed that thing to the side of the barn!*"

During the standoff with the town fathers and my uncle, every Friday Sam went to the village to meet with Joe Feree. Mr. Feree never said much when he was away from the other town fathers. Uncle Sam was careful not to say anything that would have made Joe angry. So uncle and Mr. Feree just talked about other stuff.

Late every Friday Uncle Sam would come home and stretch out on the floor of the hogan, and in the morning I'd find him with his arms across his face. Every time it was the same thing.

It was a long and agonizing wait, this standoff between the town fathers and my Uncle Sam. And little we know that Joe Feree and the town fathers were meeting secretly to weasel out an excuse to say our half-built barn had now become a nuisance to the community.

⊶⊷

The order to cease building led to unrest in the Colony. Now with the town fathers claiming the half-built barn was a community nuisance, Uncle Sam was catching it from every side. The English claimed the unrest came about in the first place because young Pequea Sam had become greedy and was treading on the toes of wannabe leaders like Joe Feree.

But really it was the jealousy of the English people bucking heads with other English. One group was concerned with what they called "Sam Fisher's greed." The rest had already caved in to the "Green-Eyed Monster Envy."

Members of the local Indian tribe vented their frustration as well. "The young white man sits on such a large chunk of what we consider our woodland. We fear that he is driving us ever closer to the reservation!"

Meanwhile, some of Uncle Sam's fellow Amish people were not happy with the formally written *Order to Cease and Desist* in the first place. These were now bothered that the community's "nuisance claim" was hurting their *image!* Both blamed the unrest on Pequea Sam's *hochmut* (highmindedness). Uncle Sam got very little sympathy from his own church people.

Now this particular controversy was beginning to carry over into the church within the Colony, the harshest of all judges, Sam felt hopeless in this newest of his tangled-up "messes." Pequea Sam was destined to watch the Fates play this one out!

⊷═◉ ◉═⊷

To begin with, Father Jacob had followed Uncle Sam to the New World. There Sam was already thriving – clearing land for more tilling and producing more crops, busily laying out farms. In the New World, the people referred to him as "Pequea Sam" because of his powerful influence throughout the Pequea area. For the brothers, one slight and fair-haired; the other one large and swarthy, thrown together in this matter in a New World, brought out their true colors.

The slight and fair-haired one had always struggled for position against the large and swarthy one, as though it was necessary to bully the other in order to get his own way. His true color was most pronounced when the slight one decided that he had to exercise a so-called "leadership" of a false power over his large and swarthy brother, a self-righteous power which would ultimately point to his own cruel death!

⊷═◉ ◉═⊷

Pequea Sam was in many ways a tragic hero. It was when the young man had to deal with his fellowman one-on-one that he had to struggle the hardest to keep his mental sickness hidden. For him, as with others, respectability was the watchword – lose control and you lose respectability, leaving you with no certain tools.

Sam was oppressed with a driving inner need to be both respected and successful. This was perhaps his tragic flaw. "It is the nature of man to rise to greatness when greatness is expected of him," maintained a famous writer. Greatness was expected of

Sam, and he was passionate to rise to what was expected of him. Same with the strictures of his church and community.

"If a man does not keep pace with his companions, perhaps it is because he hears a different drummer," wrote another famous writer. "Let him step to the music he hears, however measured or far away!"

Jacob, however, entered to the New World obsessed with a self-righteous desire for a strong and unified church brotherhood. For a visible man like Jacob, however, squeezed on all sides, the Ordnung was both a blessing and a curse. He had a secret other self that dragged a lot of skeletons and hidden agendas from the Old Country over to the New World, hard as he tried to leave them behind. His constant denial kept him constantly on edge.

On the other hand Pequea Sam desired individual prosperity above everything, along with wealth and independence and the right to be let alone. "The greater a man's 'self-proclaimed' piety, the more present his tempter. Man is, after all, subject to every temptation common to natural man." Under such a posture of self-righteousness, however, young Sam was not able to recognize his own shortcomings. Thus he remained in constant struggle between two forces: the well-intentioned good of a pioneer spirit against an ever-present *Ordnung*. He did not do well in the church.

⊷══⊙ ⊙══⊶

Coming into the New World, Jacob Fisher (Father Jacob) wanted with all his being to start with a clean slate by making one more conscious effort at trying to accept and forgive his brother Sam. However, he was found himself face-to-face with yet another demon: envy over the enormous prosperity that had followed his brother since the day he had come to the New World some years earlier. Jacob did his best to hide his envy but was often stressed by it. Finally, plagued by the envy and then saddled by own legalism as well, Father Jacob found it increasingly difficult to preach or even to shepherd his flock in the New World.

Nor was Father Jacob getting any help from my mother. My mother's greatest fear was that she had lost her former self-identity by suddenly moving half a world apart from all her former friends in the Old Country. "There is nothing here that holds us to our former identity!"

"But we are now in the New World," Father Jacob would always come back. "Our identity start here!"

⋯⇒◯ ◯⇐⋯

As to Uncle Sam, my mother had earlier on established her "position" to all. "Of course we forgave him. Forgave him a long time ago! If we had *not* forgiven him, neither would the Lord in Heaven forgive *us!* So who are we *not* to forgive *anybody?*" That's as far as it went with Mother-- from her lips and never from her heart!

⋯⇒◯ ◯⇐⋯

There were a few times when Father Jacob came close to owning up to his "double-mindedness" and the belief that he might actually be "unstable in all his ways" like it said in the Book of James. In such moments, Jacob had doubts that God even loved him at all, in turn he felt too ashamed even to "love himself." The abiding shame slowly turned into self-hatred - a driving, self-mutilating self-hatred!

⋯⇒◯ ◯⇐⋯

In the Old Country, Father Jacob had lived his life in quietness and tranquility, "under God's providence and protection." The young man had become the most highly esteemed preacher in all the Lowlands. In every gathering he reaped the authority due a man of such esteem. Even the *ausricher* (outsider) looked upon Jacob Fisher an example to emulate.

However, with time Jacob began to agonize over how to pray for and shepherd his beloved flock in the Old Country. He wasted away in contrition over the consequence of losing the *Blessing of the Forefathers* that, though tainted, he declared was rightfully his.

Meanwhile, the young preacher realized how hard his brother Sam was struggling to prove himself worthy of the *Blessing* that he had himself had "tainted." However, more than anything, Jacob struggled with the desire for revenge against his brother, so much that an ingrained bitterness would not *allow* him to forgive his brother.

Moreover, Jacob had married a contentious woman. Annie was haughty and self-righteous, always trying to "fix someone else!" She could be viciously standoffish and judgmental. Annie could get what she wanted simply by asserting herself and whining until she got her way. The wags in the church community marveled at how such opposites as Annie and Jacob Fisher had ever found each other. "Not much a man can do with a wife whose mission it is to be *church busybody!*"

Alas, Annie carried an injurious spirit with her from the Old Country to the New World. She had an ingrained habit of coughing and scratching her right palm where she imagined it itched every time she was nervous, a gesture that got her plenty of attention, but she thought was impossible to control.

"We came to the New World to live simple," Annie murmured. "To love, to reach forth, and to keep up the spirit of family and *bruderhof.* But your brother Sam destroys our dream by sinning the sin of greed."

"He's hanging us by his own hangups," she often said of Sam's "sickness."

Part Three
The Church In
The Colony

Chapter 11

Father Jacob's Pequea Church

Rest and unity prevailed in the Colony's small but growing church they referred to as the Pequea District. The love of God and fellow man was evident, and unity was a potentially powerful thing. Jacob Fisher, now a/k/a to many as Father Jacob, and his family had sustantially added to the congregation in the District. Before coming to the New World, Father Jacob started out to be a devout preacher. He was considered by everyone to be an "old fashioned *Alte Landt preacher*, a staid legalist with personal character beyond reproach.

His sensitive conscience was concerned with all matters of the church. Often he would weep over his beloved church, like the Master wept over Jerusalem. He relied on the word of God to buttress his legalism. Everyday he memorized Scriptures and recited the verses to himself, mingling them with his own supplication, with tears and groans that could not be uttered.

Father Jacob's belief was simple: *"Man should not make for himself more necessities than God has already made for him, which are not many."* His personal "credo" was simple as well: *"I am fully assured that God does not require more of any man than to believe the Scripture to be His Word, to endeavor to search for the true sense of it and then to live by it."*

Finally Sam Fisher had begun to feel a sense of vindication, like now he was finally becoming worthy of the *Blessing of the Forefathers.* At last he would be "spiritually validated" – as though his life finally stood for something and to possess some sort of value!

However, for Sam, so spiritually in tune with his Creator, life was suddenly became like the *parable of the cleanly-swept house*, wherein his demons arrive to visit and find the house was clean and empty. The demons then returned and brought with them seven new ones, so that they overwhelmed the cleanly-kept house. That's how it was for Sam Fisher. Doubts arose from everywhere and his faith began to waver.

⊷⧉ ⧉⊶

The status quo of the church was rest and commonality when Father Jacob came to it from *Das Alte Landt.* He had come as a *staid legalist who feared an angry God.* "Divine wisdom has prescribed forms of prayer," he said. "Only by *reading* a prayer is the mind quickened and the voice proclaims the God we worship."

Father Jacob's legalistic stance was at opposite poles from that of his brother. Samuel was emotional and charismatic, and spoke often with a forgiving God like one would a "Best Friend." Samuel further buttressed his stance by Billy Penn's famous statement: "I abhor two principles of religion, and pity those that own them. The first is obedience to authority without conviction; the other is destroying them that differ for God's sake."

Despite the varying bodies of thought, the congregation in the Colony managed to stay closely-knit. Everyone reached forth to help the other. If there was a need, word traveled rapidly. The needy person got the help he needed, readily and swiftly. However, there was often a price the needy one had to pay. Once a person's "neediness" became public knowledge, he gave up his right to privacy and his right to be let alone.

Over time, those same "watchful" members squabbled and threatened the rest and commonality of Father Jacob's "Church in the Colony."

⊷⇒ ⇐⊶

Father Jacob and his church started out being "concerned for the lost" but only for those lost within their own *bruderhof* or brotherhood. As for the Indians, they wrote them off as "savage" or "heathen" and did not speak of them in terms of carrying any "spiritual burden" for them. Furthermore they were intimidated by the "English" people, judged them as "this worldly" and not to be patterned after.

It was characteristic for a closed community like the Amish in the Pequea to stick close to their edicts. They stuck to them for all they were worth in order to keep them strong internally. This unity did indeed provide internal strength for the body. However that same internal *strength* was constantly eroded by its own internal *strife*, by too much church bickering.

Much of the bickering, leading to church unrest and confusion, came from people "policing" each other and by malicious talk among the women. That led to the infighting that weakened the Colony church from the inside out. As a result the people of the Colony were too busy bickering to expand its horizons wide enough to reach the *ausricher* (outsider).

At the outset, the nature of Father Jacob's *Church in the Colony* was to stress expansion of the body "from within." The church demanded a strict *Ordnung* for the members and encouraged large families. Having a lot of children was an esteemed thing, and "happy was the man whose quiver was full of them."

⊷⟫⟨⟨⟵

By far the biggest "internal" threat to the church had to do with highmindedness *(hochmut),* along with breaking the commandment against idolatry and false images.

Said the precocious Sammy II: Rather than worry about *big people stuff,* like the so-called "threats" to the church, I was far more excited in doing what tempted a normal 12-year-old, in whatever would keep his gwunnernoss adventurous and wide-eyed; such as playing in the inner woods, aimlessly wandering around in the village, nosing around in the pawnshop in the city, or just hanging out with Little Big Heart. I never knew lately what was going down with Uncle Sam and the Painted Lady, knowing that he "passed her off" as being his "head doctor."

"In any case, I was never all that affected by all the talk about threats and hochmut *so long as I was able to walk in Uncle Sam's tracks!"*

⊷⟫⟨⟨⟵

There came a time when I myself got to worrying about every little detail, mostly about Father Jacob! I was sad about seeing my loving pop so unhappy so much of the time. Seems like he had begun to grow more and more critical, especially about matters having with his church people, that he ended up drawing a lot of criticism upon *himself!*

Seems like my pop was always getting caught in some kind of old mix up or new disagreement with *somebody.* It was like he was mixing everybody together into "a very large bowl"--into a large antagonist *crucible* as some people called it – with anybody my pop disagreed with or found himself to be "at odds" with.

Chapter 12

The Antagonist Crucible

First of all, Father Jacob found himself in the *crucible* was with his charismatic brother, my Uncle Sam, over how prayers were to be uttered in church. From there it was with the "English" people who had been turning far too "this worldly." Then is was with the Native American people after my mother Annie had collectively written them off – lock, stock and barrel --as a bunch of *heathens* or *savages*.

Finally Father Jacob found himself in an "antagonist crucible" of sorts with members of his precious church, caught in a heated disagreement over who should have the final say over matters related to the *Ordnung*.

⊷⊐◖ ◗⊐⊶

In the *crucible* with his own brother Sam. The more emotional of the Fisher brothers, Uncle Sam was critical of how his brother conducted prayers in the church. Jacob, a staid legalist, had mandated that every prayer be read from a black prayer book he had brought with him from the Old Country. *"Personal wisdom comes by reading a prayer, wherein the mind is quickened and the voice ever proclaims the God we worship,"* said Father Jacob who memorized most of the short prayers, simply because he had read them so often. Some referred to Father Jacob as "Man with the gift of memory."

For the charismatic (Pentecostal) Sam it was a different matter. "*Divine wisdom*," he said, "comes from *reciting* a prayer, wherein the mind is quickened by the actual sound of the voice, whereby the uttered words ever proclaim the God we worship."

For the "emotionalist" Sam Fisher, earnest prayer had already begun inside the Catacombs. There he had to learn what he had to do in order to survive, namely to love God and neighbor; to bless and not to curse. For Sam, earnest prayer had begun by memorizing the words of the Psalmist, then reciting the words back to his Creator, like the Psalmist did.

And so it was that all up and down the Pequea, by Father Jacob's edict, prayers had to be read from the little black book which he had brought with him from *Das Alte Landt*. Silent prayer was to remain silent at all times.

⤝⭢ ⭠⤞

In the *crucible* with the English people and the Quakers. Father Jacob and his church were intimidated by the New World "English" and judged them as far too "this worldly" and not to be patterned after. Moreover, when the present English first heard that a folk called "Amish" were coming from the Old Country to settle in Penn's Woods, they were not comfortable, much less comfortable with their "critical and far too opinionated" young leader and preacher. Many of the English people were bent upon discouraging the Amish process by talking it into the ground. Neither Father Jacob nor "Fix-it Annie" were happy about this.

Nevertheless those same English people watched closely the Amish process in the making. One day at a time, one frolic at a time, one season at a time, while the wilderness was pushed back and became a paradise. The doomsayers could never have imagined that one day their quiet neighbors would carve the "Garden Spot of America" out of a once-hostile woodland.

As to the Quakers, even though the Amish and the Quakers thought a lot in common, Jacob and his church considered the Quakers too progressive, too modern, too attuned with the things of this world. So with the Quakers, Father Jacob justified his basic tenet, *separation from the world,* by deliberately "standing apart!" This in turned many of the Quakers the wrong way.

In the *crucible* with the Native American people. In dealing with the Indians already in Pennsylvania, Billy Penn had two chief concerns: establishing trade and gaining title to land in a peaceful manner. *"Indians and English must live together in love as long as the sun gives light,"* he mandated. *"My grantees must not affront, nor in any way wrong, any Native American under penalty of law."* As for the Indians, the church did not speak of them in terms of carrying any "spiritual burden" for them. This was undoubtedly out of ignorance and fear, after the colonial people "stretched" too many stories they had heard about this so-called "savage people!" Therefore, Father Jacob and a lot of his church members, especially his wife Annie, wrote the Native American off as "savage" or "heathen" *across the board.* Needless to mention, this was certainly not the case with Pequea Sam!

As far as being in a *crucible* with his own church, Father Jacob had become so self-righteous and protective of his own personal opinions that he found himself at odds with many of the members of his own precious church. His chief controversy, mainly personal, started over who should have the final say over matters related to the *Ordnung* within the church body.

Other than this chief controversy, one minor controversy had a way of leading into another until the leader found himself hopelessly entangled with member after member. At times a member would watch a disagreement start with a rather insignificant matter, then jump into the mess, only to watch a petty matter blow out of proportion just for the sake of more in-fighting. Thus did the shepherd lead his flock into the very same *crucible!*

⊷══ ══⊶

"The Antagonist Crucible District" is what the people quickly bandied about, over back fences or at frolics, by busybodies from the other Pequea Church district. As well as the people knew how, the talk about Father Jacob and his church stayed hushed and stayed tight within the Colony. The settlement managed to keep their private matters, especially any infighting, strictly private, away from the criticism of their English neighbors.

The stoic people within the settlement were prone to "fight like cats and dogs." However, these same people shied away from ever letting their personal conflicts and "very private in-fighting" leak out to others!

⊷══ ══⊶

Far more subtle and insidious, however, was Jacob's "entanglement" with yet another member of his church. "Rascal John" was the so-called "Trickster" of the church, one who delighted in upsetting whatever was the present status quo. Here was a rascal member who stirred up trouble just for the sake of doing it!

The rascal, or trickster, was ever inclined to differ with whatever happened to be the status quo within of the Colony church. No matter what the status quo, the rascal did his level best to upset *anything* that came along!

It was fairly obvious that Rascal John was so preoccupied with trying to upset matters that he had little time to look out for his own things. The rascal member longed for esteem in the church and credibility in his community in order to cover his hidden faults. However, his double life, followed his own guilt over his own hidden faults got in his way.

Rascal John, a great pretender, was able to cover a multitude of his own hidden faults by informing his church leader of the petty transgressions of others. In turn Father Jacob, himself a great pretender, tried to hide his secret sin against his brother Samuel, along with his abiding sin of unforgiveness by being a stern leader.

In the church service, the Rascal tried to be the pillar in the church. Most thought he was, including himself. The church wags and busybodies claimed that the rascal's "piety" was driven by "remorse," and that he was "ever repenting the sins of his youth."

Rascal John looked askance upon even the most pious members of the body, wreaking to stir up mischief about them as well. He rode the trolley to the city just to see who may have been riding on it, inclined to spot anybody doing something he thought was other than normal; even to detect who had been riding the trolley frequently so he could report his finding and his suspicions to Father Jacob.

"Nice day, indeed it is," the Rascal responded to the painted lady seated on her stoop, surprising him as he walked by her "exceedingly-wicked establishment!" He responded to the "lady" much more fondly than his "holy will power" meant to after he experienced a tinge of excitement. He deliberately walked by the place the second time. She was no longer there.

Returning home on the trolley, he recalled the painted lady on her stoop. Seeing her had giving him "the shivers!" Somehow the Rascal in his newly-found "excitement" knew he would be going up that very same street. *Very soon!* "Just to see who might be hanging around the frowned-upon area. *For no other reason!*"

My pop and the Rascal were often seen talking rather earnestly together, especially at the barn raising where they stayed to themselves in order to deal with matters that were seeming to cause my father pain.

I began putting together bits and pieces of *rascal gossip* whenever I got close enough to hear what he was telling my pop. "Now don't you bother yourself with stuff we talk about," said my father after Uncle Sam's barn raising. "Next thing you'll know more than is good for you!"

"As if I don't know too much already!"

⋅►═◄ ►═◄⋅

My Uncle Sam is the best singer of anybody in the whole church district. *"Because he sings so well, everybody thinks he's the staunchest man in the district."* He holds this high status by carrying a solemn Sunday demeanor. Even the children who sit near to Uncle Sam behave themselves better during the church service for fear of "offending" this upstanding man of the church.

⋅►═◄ ►═◄⋅

Uncle Sam had become a weasler of sorts, one who had over time learned to "dance in all worlds." He could appear pious and therefore stay out of the "Ordnung spotlight." He practiced the rules of Ordnung carefully, especially those having to the dress retriction, always careful not to make to a spectacle of himself. The way that a man dressed and kept himself spoke a lot about the kind of man he was. Pequea Sam knew that, and so that behind a feigned piety he could get by with a multitude of trangressions. He knew that although piety could hide a multitude of sins, it could also roll back and bite the one who relied on it solely for spiritual strength.

⇢══ ══⇠

Uncle Sam was a "driven man" with a finely tuned sense of sin. To him, idleness was a form of sin. The aversion he felt for idleness of any sort, kept him on edge, driven and restless. On a day he was not working because he was depressed, he had an especially rough battle with his own sins, both the generational sin against his brother, Father Jacob, or with every other of sin that came along.

Uncle Sam arrived at church early. Almost always he was the first one there. He kept to himself, another outward sign of his solemn Sabbath demeanor. He also left early, because it was his day to be alone, to think. I suppose he is fighting to keep up the reputation of being the most successful Amish man in the Colony.

"Every day I watch my Uncle Sam prosper. I pray that it might continue, in spite of the two faces he is always wearing!"

⇢══ ══⇠

My father Jacob minds his own business. He does not talk much about religion. To him somebody's religion, "especially your own," was not anything you talked about. It was too personal, far too private. "What is there to talk about in the first place?" my pop always used to say. "If you already believe in something, what business does anybody have to get you to believe something else? My relationship with the Almighty is my own business, not something I even need to talk about. I don't even talk about this to my own family!"

"Rascal John is much too busy tattling about other people's business! His list must be getting so long I'm afraid it's just a matter of time 'til he starts tattling stuff about Uncle Sam. I worry about that every time I see the ole rascal "buttering up" my pop!"

⊷══ ══⊶

Father Jacob constantly struggled with an inner conflict of still another kind I never knew about. It seems that he had never forgiven my Uncle Samuel for "tainting" the *blessing of the forefathers*. The conflict had already plagued Jacob as a sensitive lad growing up in *Das Alte Landt*. This same old conflict escalated after Jacob first arrived in the New World to join up with his then-estranged brother.

As a youth Jacob found it almost impossible to forgive my Uncle Samuel because he had wasted all of his childhood years harboring his bitterness. As an adult, he struggled even harder to forgive but still could not do it. Deep down, he doubted that his sin was even "forgiveable!" He had followed an ingrained teaching that blasphemy against the Holy Ghost was an abomination, making any such transgression simply "unpardonable."

Jacob had long forgiven his brother "in his mind" but then could not get it together in his heart. So he travailed in angry silence with a spirit bent on revenge. To that end the young man became grew more and more "spiritually unstable." He knew that although piety could hide a multitude of sins, it could also roll back and bite the one who relied on it solely for spiritual strength.

Chapter 13

The Doctrines of the Church

C hurch Doctrine was strictly adhered to, both in *Das Alte Landt* and in the New World, where Jacob Fisher would now be at the helm. Under the church's main doctrine there were several time-honored observances. ORDNITZ GMAY (*To review the church's Ordnung*) and GROSS GMAY (*Sacred Communion*) were among the chief observances. Held every spring and then again during every fall, there was no getting out of these, short of being strofed before the entire church body. If the need arose, there would be other observances, such as were necessary to carry out of the business of a church's district or in case of general emergency. These consisted mostly to issues around stofing, ex-commuication and the like.

Sitz Gmay

Jacob Fisher, known as Father Jacob to his budding young son, was the leader of the Pequea District. Father Jacob was in charge of *sitz gmay* (literally "to stay seated past the main service.") A service with a heart of its own, *Sitz gmay* was for baptized members only. It was preserved for members in good standing with the church congregation to decide what to do with those who been recently *strofed.*

The service was set aside for taking care of the so-called "business matters" of the church body, which included discipling and sometime expeling, those members who had strayed too far from the *Ordnung*.

Today Father Jacob had on his most somber face. The "trial" of his very own flesh-and-blood lay onerously upon his shoulders. To be passing judgment, both before God and all of mankind, on his own brother, left the church leader "mortally naked" and afraid. His hand remained fixed upon his breast, a sign to every member in the church body of the heaviness of the sacred duty placed upon their young leader.

Sammy II, conspicuous by his absence, snuck off into the woods to look for Little Big Heart after picking up a slew of negative vibes, more than his small mind could sort out, surrounding his cherished uncle. Meawhile, back in the shed the service continued.

The onus had instantly spread throughout Father Jacob's flock. Every eye remained fixed ahead and downward. No one uttered a sound except for an occasional cough. Now and then a crumpled hankie gathered in a muffled sniffle. Father Jacob gnawed at his lower lip to indicate his deep disturbance.

Young Sam Fisher sat with his head down and eyes closed as though in prayer. His face burned like hot washrags pressing into his cheeks. His temples pounded in the silence. But his mind stayed firmly fixed on the "sins" for which he was about "stand trial."

Jacob pronounced the charge against his brother, after which "the fallen one" was allowed to utter his own words.

"We create a so-called Ordnung and place it above the very one who created us. We think we must always DO. We never take the time just to BE! Every test in life makes us either bitter or better. Every problem comes to make us or break us. The choice is ours whether we become victim or victor."

"He blasphemeth!"

"Salvation is not about reaching up to the Almighty and saying how much you love Him. It's about Him reaching down to love us, saint and sinner alike. It's not about how good we are and how strictly we follow the rules; it's about God loving us, no matter what. It's not about anything we try to give to the Almighty to please Him. It's about God giving to man!"

"He must speak no further!"

"Even a fool is considered wise when he holds his peace!" Sam recalled the madam's words vividly."*We cast aside the commands of the Almighty in order to hold onto the traditions of man, such as we do in "Mark chapter seven!" said the fearless Pequea Sam, hanging onto his last thread to keep from going under.*

And then came the overarching question: "Who bans this brother from the Body and the Blood?"

One by one, as though fearing reprisal, they utter, "Yes, I am as one with the controversy." No one looks up to say their piece.

Rascal John remained silent. Following a long, ear-piercing silence, the congregation awaited the Rascal's voice, the last remaining vote to make the "verdict" unanimous.

The Rascal's words broke the silence. "The brother makes his bed in whoredom!"

The verdict falls, without further question from "the newly-fallen one."

The Strofing

Pequea Sam had been treading on mighty thin ice with the church after Joe Feree issued the Order to stop building and nailed it on the side of our half-built barn. Then came the town fathers claiming the half-built barn was a "nuisance to the community." The church elders decided that Sam was not separating himself from the outside world, rather he was conflicting with those who were already of this world. Now he had to be *strofed* (admonished by the entire church body).

The *strofing* was a somber occasion, held after a regular church service, but separate from the main service. The occasion was for baptized members only. Having to *strofe* Sam, his own blood brother, saddened Father Jacob deeply, filling his eyes with tears and every member's eyes as well. The young preacher kept his eyes lowered the entire time of the *strofing*.

Said Sam when he was called in front of the church body. "The Master gave his life because of our wrongdoing, and now He has something to say about how we conduct our lives, *the very life of His church,* about loving God and neighbor, and about not judging fellowman."

Stone silence.

"Our Lord God is not about a lot of rules and a bunch of do's and do not's. He is about relationship, about how I conduct my life and connect with Him and His people. However, we won't give up our rules – our do's and do not's – for fear we have no way to control each other."

Deafening silence.

Despite fighting for all he was worth, the congregation "votes" in silent anonymity, and so the die is cast. Sam is somberly and mystically admonished by his peers and departs from the congregation in the deafening silence.

Jacob is mortally naked and afraid. His hand clings tightly to his breast.

Preparatory Service

At the *preparatory service*, which was observed two Sundays before *Sacred Communion,* all signs of mirth and laughter were gone from Jacob's eyes. He kept his head lowered at all times. Obviously he was *out of it!* Sometimes when spoken to, he did not respond at all – like he was not able to! At the slightest provocation his hand immediately found his heart.

The preparatory service was meant to be a happy occasion in anticipation of those who were being invited to participate in the Lord's Table. However, *the man with the gift of memory* did not smile. His eyes remained at all times downcast; he appeared so *out of it!*

"Sinners are to be held accountable to their God for their transgressions. The Lord our God is forgiving, but He also punishes. To simply say "I'm sorry" every time you commit a sin, is not the acceptable way to heaven. There must be no "shortcut to the Promised Land!"

Sacred Communion

It was Fall Communion Day. The day of final reckoning had arrived. For Samuel Fisher, nothing compared to the sacredness of the Lord's Table at Sacred Communion. *"Give yourselves up to the church's Ordnung. Give up your prideful way of life. Give up your feeble right to avenge yourselves"* were among the lastest congregrational edicts.

Young Samuel was still under the *strofing* from the preparatory service two weeks before when word about consorting with a brothel madam trickled throughout Jacob's congregation. Once more the young man thought he had to fight for his very life against the stiff judgment of his brother and his congregation, the harshest possible "trial" before his peers.

It was a Sunday morning like all others up and down the Pequea Colony, quiet and unassuming. Still it was like no other. Clouds of anxiety hung in the air, ready to attack anyone who would give in to the angst. Even the children sensed the tension as they left their designated positions and single-filed out of the shed after the main service. The time of reckoning had arrived for the man they called Pequea Sam.

Ex-Communication

"We hold one another accountable to lead Christian lives. Sometimes we have to excommunicate one of our own, to expel him from the membership, to compel the unrepentant to mend his way."

The *strofing,* followed by the *excommunication,* were by far the hardest on Father Jacob. Here was the most severe test of the spirit the young preacher could ever have faced. This would be the most difficult duty to carry out among the members of the Pequea District, no matter who was being excommunicated. Now the duty had to do with the very flesh and blood that Father Jacob has once been attached to even before birth, whose heel he then came forth grabbing.

Pequea Sam felt as though he had just experienced something apart from his senses. He had to watch it unfold through everyone else's eyes, then walked away from the shed a *newly-fallen man.*

As he walked out, eyes here and there lifted hesitantly and followed the newly-fallen man out. Some merely exchanged glances, wondering what each would have dared say, in defense of the *fallen*, if they had been permitted to talk. A dull anger pulses down inside his gut, pulling his spirit still further down. He walked home without eating or even talking with the members.

Handfuls of men quietly gathered around a long table made from propped-up benches for the *Fellowship Meal.* No one spoke. In the kitchen the women stood frozen.

After the excommunication, Samuel's place would no longer be a place where people gathered to socialize. No one would any longer to be inclined to consider his place to do business. Sam's place would no longer be friendly and open to the church members. The public as well would sense the tension and shy away for a long time.

Excommunication had its own way of doing that.

Chapter 14

Violation of the Temple

When "the search party" came upon the deceased, the edges of a grisly, crudely hand-done "tattoo" had already begun turning into a vile green. The "raw flesh" crawled in its own "pain." Several of those unable were to continue looking on. Those sensed a violation so overpowering that they virtually imagined "touching" the evil; "smelling" the evil!

The remaining members of the "search party" were left to decifer similar marks the violator had used to violate his chest and belly areas. Some of the markings had long since healed, leaving others who were looking on to second guess what the original marking may have meant to infer. *"Sam?" "Forgive?" "Death?"*

Each one of the late Father Jacob's various markings made sense only to the eye of the beholder.

Chapter 15

The Colony "Grabhof"

T he black-shrouded procession traipsed in single file past the "Hangin' Tree," down the narrow, weed-grown path to the Colony *Grabhof* (graveyard). The men in front walked in quiet surrender, following by the women and the several children, according to age and family.

The *solemn committee* had already reached their *agreement* by lot: that the self-mutilation of the deceased was a fatal infliction upon one of God's own children, an violation of the Temple of the Most High God, an ingregious act without redemption. So they buried the subject *outside of* the graveyard fence.

The solemn procession stopped short of a heavy whitewashed wooden gate and gathered around a lone, freshly-dug grave just *outside of* the entrance. The Old Order custom of banning murderers and self-mutilators from the Colony Grabhof had begun in the Old Country and followed the folk to the New World.

The silent procession stopped short of the whitewashed gate. One final time the family members gathered around the a lone grave *outside of* the entrance of the Grabhof. The closest family members stopped momentarily to take the last look inside the simple wooden pine box.

The thumping of clods on and around the simple pine box had already begun by the time the last of the procession had reached the grave. The burial was over in short order, as it was for one who died outside of God's grace.

At the very end of the solemn procession came the excommunicated Pequea Sam. He hurried right past Father Jacob's humble wood coffin, trying to preserve his brother's spirit by not even looking down at his corpse.

Chapter 16

Return of the Madam

ammy II and Little Big Heart hurried to tell the madam what they had seen. As the two were returning from the graveyard, Pequea Sam suddenly seemed to disappear from sight. "We followed him as far as the Prayin' Tree. We were going to keep our eyes on him! We thought we were being very careful not to let him get out of our sight!"

"Aren't we blessed to put the matter into the Creator's hands and let him sort things in His way?" pondered the madam. "A man can die and the nation ring with praise for what he was; while just beneath, it rings with gladness that he is dead. God calls men to heavy reckoning for overweening pride. Furthermore, according to Greek tragedy all arrogance must one day reap a harvest of tears," the madam continued to philosophize.

Chapter 17

The "Hangin' Tree"

Pequea Sam hastened from the Colony Grabhof to hide in the crotch of the 'Hangin' Tree.' *"Who am I not to forgive my brother?"*

"As for me, my good and noble brother, it was not the dying that hurt, as much as dying for nothing. Why did you have to choose such a grimy and permanent end to a temporary situation? Why, Jacob?"

He looked down at the abundant water of the Pequea, and at all the rich limestone soil that he had turned into his very own land *flowing with milk and honey,* in keeping with Billy Penn's "Holy Experiment."

Pequea Sam Fisher was mighty proud of his farm ground. Sam and his little *knecht* Sammy II had labored to turn their little farm into a few tillable acres. In time, a big-hearted Susquehannock a/k/a Grosse Hartz, along with his young son, Little Big Heart, had helped him to turn a virgin forest into what had ultimately worked together for the everybody's good!

As Pequea Sam pondered all of these matters in his mind from high in the branches, he recalled vividly the last words of the towering Susquehannock, Big Heart, as he quoted his ancient Apache warrior, Chief Geronimo. *"There is one God looking down on us all. We are all the children of one God. The sun, the darkness, the winds are all listening to what we have to say!"*

"One thing for certain," asserted Pequea Sam, *"The Good Lord in His mercy has showered upon me all the blessings I am able to contain! Thank you, Lord!"*

FINALE

Epilogue

P.S. Author's Apology

I confess to the many writing errors – spelling, formatting and such –throughout this book. I will explain why, by your grace. A whole host of unforeseen things "blindsided" me in the process of writing and later in finishing the book.

Halfway through writing the first draft, I suffered a paralyzing stroke following heart surgery. I lost the use of my entire right side and had to "start over" – like learning to *write* left-handed, *think* right-brained, and *type* with one finger – *starting over big time!* However, I was determined to finish the book, despite my "setback" and grappling with bouts of depression and feeling somewhat helpless. Had it not been for Rachel Goldberg, Staff Member at the Life Care Center at Hilo (Hawaii), I might not have had the courage to start over and continue writing, much less to *complete* the book!

Forgiving myself for the stroke, keeping my head above the water, and "finding my way" a second time – was a difficult thing to accomplish! But Rachel literally "became my virtual brains" and walked me through the process. I could never have accomplished it otherwise. Rachel Goldberg is truly a proverbial "Angel of Mercy" – one who performs beyond the call of duty to help others. *Rachel deserves the highest praise!*

Finally, the "unforeseen" notwithstanding, the book is out. *Hallelujah!*

J. B. Fisher